LESTER SCHWINGLE

PLEASE RETURN
IN 2 WKS.

LUCKY

THE YOUNG SOLDIER

By

ELMER SHERWOOD

Author of "Lucky, the Boy
Scout", "Buffalo Bill", etc.

Illustrations by Neil O'Keeffe

WHITMAN PUBLISHING Co.
RACINE • • CHICAGO

TABLE OF CONTENTS

LIST OF ILLUSTRATIONS

This Book Is Dedicated to Two Boys Who Are the Main Inspiration of this Story

LUCKY, THE
YOUNG
SOLDIER

Lucky, the Young Soldier

CHAPTER I

SYD GRAHAM'S INVITATION

"I WISH I could go," said Ted. "You fel-fellows are going to have a world of fun."

Syd Graham's face showed his disappointment. Ted was quick to notice this.

"I'm sorry, Syd. Don't think for a moment I don't want to go." And Ted Marsh turned and put his hands on his chum's shoulders. It hurt him to know how disappointed Syd was; at the same time he felt proud that he would be missed so much.

Seven boys were in comfortable possession of Syd Graham's room. He had called them together to extend the invitation to his home

15

for the coming vacation and had outlined his plan for camping, boating and fishing. He had obtained permission from his father—Colonel Graham. All the boys but Ted Marsh had accepted. The boys were specially happy over the fact that Syd's father had given his consent, for it made their own parents' approval so much the more likely.

But for Syd, half of the anticipation and joy of the party was gone. He was genuinely attached to Ted. Truth to confess, the inspiration of the party had come to him because he wanted Ted with him during vacation.

"What keeps you from going, Ted?" inquired Tom Walker, one of the boys in the room, who had noticed Syd's disappointment. "Can you tell us?" he added.

"I can only tell you what I know," replied Ted. "This morning I received a letter from Mack who is down at the Double X Ranch, asking me not to promise to go anywhere, vacation time. That's all I know about it."

"Then there is a chance of your being able to come, isn't there?" broke in Syd hopefully.

"Not much, I guess, for Mack is coming up next week to Wayland," was Ted's answer. "If he considers it important enough to come up here, he must have a definite plan in mind."

Some of the other boys were already discussing the trip and the coming vacation. School was in its closing month. It had been an interesting year at Wayland Academy, yet all of the boys were looking vacation-ward.

For Ted, the year had been an especially fruitful one. He had made many friends; he was respected and admired. Beside his gift of born leadership, he had many likable qualities that endeared him to everyone who knew him. He had proved his ability and courage the year before, through experiences that had been the means of developing him.

"You talk as if you were preparing to go to a girl's birthday party, Earl. Remember that this trip is a camping trip and the fewer clothes you take the better." Tom Walker prided himself on his knowledge of camping and its necessities and he was poking fun at Earl Thorson who was planning to take a number of things with him.

The talk continued on the amount necessary to pay all the expenses.

Perhaps this is as good a time as any to give a brief account of the adventures of Lucky, the Boy Scout, adventures which are familiar to many of our readers but with which some of them are still unacquainted.

Ted Marsh, Lucky the Boy Scout, a newsboy of Chicago, meets John Dean, a rancher from the great Northwest of Canada. He goes West with the latter where he meets Red Mack and Smiles and makes other friends. He has a number of exciting adventures and later in the story, it develops that one of his new found friends is his father, who had left home just before Ted was born. Ted goes to Wayland Academy, and because he has proved that he has a keen mind, he is sent to Chicago by a number of Canadian gentlemen on a mission of great importance. He is successful and receives a letter of commendation and one thousand dollars as reward. His mother and sister go West and the Marsh family is reunited. Ted goes back to Wayland where we find him at the beginning of our story.

The boys continued their earnest discussion and planning. Ted joined in just as eagerly as the rest though he was fairly certain that he could not be with them. He felt it was fine that the rest of the boys could go.

In the midst of the discussion, the loud clang of a bell brought the boys in a mad scuffle to the door. It was supper hour. Little time was left for them to go to their rooms, get ready, and be down at the table within the five minutes allowed. It left Ted and Syd, who were roommates, together. There was a moment's constraint between them, for Syd felt the disappointment of Ted's not going.

Ted broke it with, "I'm sorry, as I told you, Syd. I want to go, you know that."

"I know it, Ted. It's all right. Anyway, it will be nice to meet Mack, when he comes."

"It may be, but that is no reason why you should hold that brush forever. Other people have to use it, too," replied Ted teasingly.

"I will, if I want to," challenged Syd. "Come and take it if you want it."

There was a tussle for a minute, then came

the realization that they were late. They hastened downstairs laughing and in the best of humor, once again in thorough accord and understanding.

CHAPTER II

RED MACK ARRIVES

A YOUNG man, not older than twenty-seven, sauntered into the school grounds.

The big Stetson in his hand and his weather-beaten face, were fair proof of the fact that he was no effete Easterner.

He stopped one of the boys who passed him.

"Can you tell me about where I can find Ted Marsh?" he asked in a friendly manner.

"Ted Marsh?" the boy repeated, "why, I just left him at baseball practice."

"Thank you," the man replied, "that's over there, isn't it?" and he pointed to where there were many boys and the sound of voices.

The boy nodded in assent. Then, as Red Mack continued his way, Allan Mabie turned and watched him.

"That must be one of Ted's friends from the ranch," the boy decided. "Guess I'll just trot back that way and see who he is."

Red Mack reached the grounds but he saw no sign of Ted. As a matter of fact, the boy had just left.

Red Mack, his red hair flaming conspicuously, watched the boys at play without the least sign of hurry. He figured that this was as likely a spot as any to find Ted at this hour.

"Say, Syd," Allan Mabie called to Ted's chum. "Ted Marsh is wanted. This man here is asking for him."

Syd Graham turned. When he saw who the man was, he threw the ball to one of the other boys and hurried over.

"You're Mack—I mean Mr. Mack, aren't you?"

"Know me my my red hair, do you?" Red Mack quizzed, grinning broadly.

"I'd know you anywhere," the boy stoutly asserted. "I'm Ted's chum. My name is Syd Graham."

"Well, I've heard reports of you, too, young

man. Don't let me keep you from practice, though; I can wait."

"You're not keeping me," Syd replied. "Fact is, both Ted and I have been expecting you. Shall we go over to the dormitory?"

"Just as you say, Syd," Red Mack replied. "I'm in no particular hurry and I'd just as soon wait."

The need for decision, however, was removed for Ted was seen hurrying toward them. One of the boys had raced to the house and informed Ted of Red Mack's arrival.

"Hello, Red," he called when he was still far away. He waved his cap and increased his speed.

Red Mack waved back. "Hello, Ted," he called, upon the boy's nearer approach.

Though boy and man were happy in the meeting, neither let his feelings show too strongly.

The boys on the grounds watched the two, although they pretended to be busy at play or in talking to each other.

There was a few moments casual conversation, neither Mack nor the boy touching upon the subject which had prompted Red's trip.

"Hey, fellows," Ted called to the other boys. "Come over."

The boys came over, sheepishly. "This is my friend, Mr. Mack. I guess you've heard me talk of him."

"Yes, and I reckon he talked disrespectfully of me, too. Probably called me Red Mack."

The boys laughed; the man's manner was so simple, so genuinely natural, that they soon felt at home.

After a half hour on the campus, the three, Ted, Syd and Red Mack repaired to the house.

"Nice boys, those," Red Mack commented. "I like them."

Syd by this time felt as if he had known Ted's friend all his life.

He found himself explaining about the picnic he had planned. But he said nothing of his disappointment at the failure of Ted to go along. That wouldn't be sportsmanlike and Syd was true blue, consciously and unconsciously.

But Red Mack gathered from the boy's tones something of the state of affairs. However, he said nothing.

"I came down," he said, once they had seated themselves comfortably, "with a proposition which I thought would interest Ted. He, of course, is free to say whether he wants to join us or not. I don't mean to interfere with anything Ted may prefer to do. He knows me well enough to know that I want him to decide for himself."

Ted said nothing. There was a great understanding between the two; the kind which made words unnecessary.

"Well, I guess I'll tell you all about it, then you can judge and decide for yourself. Here goes—"

CHAPTER III

TED HEARS MACK'S PLAN

"IT'S nearly eight years—perhaps nine— since Smiles and I left Arizona. At that time the Mexicans were making very little trouble but nevertheless we both decided after a set-to with some of them, that mining in that vicinity wasn't particularly healthy.

"We intended to go back after a year or more—but we liked it too much at the Double X.

"Smiles is gone now.

"Your father and I, Ted, have decided to go down there. Arthur is going too. We're going to try out that mine, once for all. We'll know whether it's a fizzle or not. Arthur, Pop and I—between us. We have enough money to carry us through."

"Is mother willing to let father go?" Ted

asked with the memory of his father's long absence fresh in his mind.

"Yes, she is. She feels as Helen does," and here Red Mack flushed a deep red—"that the chance is worth while. If it brings any success, we'll all be comfortable; if it doesn't, why it's one of the chances you run in any undertaking.

"We will know the probabilities of success within three months. The Mexicans do not materialize in any great number at this point of the border; at any rate, we shall be on United States territory." Red Mack paused for a minute, then abruptly he came to his point.

"Want to come, Ted?"

"Do I want to come?" The boy whooped with joy. From his seat in the corner where he had listened, quiet but with a keen interest, Syd Graham felt a pang of disappointment. Why couldn't he have been included? Of course, it wasn't possible but nevertheless he envied his chum.

"Did you hear that, Syd? I'm to go with Red Mack to Arizona!" Ted's excitement was still intense.

"My, Syd, I wish you could come with us," he added the next second.

"It isn't going to be child's play—I can warn you. It will mean hard work and we shall expect you to do many things we'd expect a man to do. You see, we decided on you, rather than a fourth man, because we all know you can come up to the test."

"Syd's of that kind, too, Red," Ted replied in loyal defense of his friend.

"I think so, from my short acquaintance— but—" and Red Mack hesitated.

"I couldn't go, Ted," Syd interrupted. "You know I'd like to and I'm glad you want me along, but you know we have planned our party."

"That's so. I forgot about that," Ted agreed.

"And I can't blame you for holding off until hearing from Mr. Mack," Syd added.

"Well, other events are happening daily," Red Mack remarked consolingly. "When we make plans again we'll have to include Syd."

"When do you start?" Ted asked.

"School closes in ten days, doesn't it? Well, we should like to make our start in two weeks. Can you manage?" Red inquired.

"I think so," the boy answered slowly, a trifle thoughtfully. "By the way, Red, what does Mr. Dean say about your going?"

"Well, we wondered how he'd take it. Your father has made a splendid foreman. He is liked by the men and he has shown results. The boss, I know, hates to lose him, but when he learned the reason he didn't think of standing in our way. You know how square he is. A fellow can't help but be square in return.

"He has arranged for our going—won't listen to our even putting it off."

"Some of the boys at school are going to leave a little early—maybe I will, too," Ted remarked. "That will give me a little more time at home."

Syd decided at this moment that he had some business to attend to elsewhere. There was nothing calling him away but he felt that perhaps Mack and Ted would like to talk over some things in privacy.

The two friends went into further details as

to the trip. There was much to discuss, many angles to the project.

"Of course, trouble may come. The Mexicans are a treacherous lot and will make trouble, if the opportunity comes. But, it's worth the risk," Red Mack decided.

"I was wondering, Red, if you didn't want the thousand dollars I received as a reward from the Canadian Government? Do you need it?"

"Yes, we do, but we felt, your father and I, it was your money and so he decided not to touch it. Sure you want to include it in the fund?" Red Mack warned.

"Yes, I want to, very much. It may help at some time. By the way, when do you return?" the boy asked.

"Tonight, if I can make a train," Red Mack replied. "Then I'd be home in the morning."

The two repaired to the office of the school. A train was leaving at ten o'clock that night. Mr. Oglethorpe, the dean, gave both Ted and Syd permission to see their friend to the train.

Ten o'clock found Red Mack on his trip homeward. Syd and Ted had walked down to the station with him and although the hour was late they decided to walk back to the school.

The two boys talked of many things, chief of which was Red Mack. To each of them, he presented the ideal of manhood. And truth to tell, there were few men who approached more nearly the ideal—clean, active and lithe, a quick thinker, educated, but at no time using his education for exhibition. A tried man, honest, ready and loyal. At no time had Ted found him to fail in any respect.

It was of some of these things that he told Syd on their way home. He had a great loyalty for the man, and although Syd had heard the story before, he told again of Red Mack's daring in entering the cave of the outlaws, while he, Ted Marsh, had hurried for help.

"We'll have to get in quietly, won't we?" Syd remarked as they came to the dormitories.

"Yes, lights are out," Ted replied. "I'm tired, too," he added.

"So am I," Syd agreed.

CHAPTER IV

A Good Investment

THE train came to a stop at the station. Our friends, Bill Marsh, Red Mack, Arthur and Ted alighted.

It had been planned to travel light. Whatever they needed, it was decided, could be obtained at Payson, the railroad station nearest the mine. There were some things of course that had to be brought along—these had been packed in as small a space as possible.

Red Mack, Arthur and the older Marsh were old hands at the game. It was Red Mack who had decided on buying the necessary horses in Arizona. For one thing he felt that they would be acclimated. He also felt that by seemingly innocent questioning he could find an Indian or two, who would sell them the horses they needed at a low figure.

He left Arthur and the older Marsh at the station to collect their baggage. Taking Ted with him, he sought the Indian village which was about three miles from the station.

The Indians were more than ready to sell him the necessary horses, but when they found one skilled in all the tricks of horse-trading some of their eagerness departed. Red Mack, Ted watching him with great interest, drove a hard bargain. He bought two horses and two mules.

"We'll have to economize," he remarked to Ted. "We'll have all our stuff carted—and two of us will use the mules for the time being. They are needed for their strength and stamina," he added.

He then arranged with one of the Indians to do their hauling from the station.

On their return, about a mile from the station, a curious sight met their eyes. Two men were tinkering around a Ford which had evidently balked and refused to run.

"I tell you, Howard," one was telling the other—"the only thing to do with this old flivver is to leave it here—and travel the rest of the way as respectable people do. I'm sick of this. Never again."

"You're no sicker than I am, Amos," the other replied. "It was a mistake to start out. We were idiots to think we could get to Texas in 15 days. It seems wicked, however, just to leave it. Wasteful," he added.

"But look at the waste in keeping at it. Time and energy. Besides, we'll never make it in time, and the old tin isn't worth anything now, anyway."

"Hello, strangers," the first man turned and greeted Red and Ted upon their approach.

"Can I help you?" Mack inquired.

"You can if you can tell us how far the station is," the second man, Howard, replied.

"About a mile. Why, the station, however? The town is over there," and he pointed the way they had come.

The men told him their troubles and their decision to abandon the Ford. As they went into details an idea occurred to Ted. He turned to Red Mack who allowed his eyelash to quiver for a second.   Ted realized that Mack was bent on some plan and so made no suggestion.

"Of course, it may be," Red suggested, "I can repair your car; I'd be glad to, if I can," he offered.

"No thank you," one of the men replied. "We'd rather settle the matter at this point than twenty miles from a station."

"I'll tell you what I'll do, friends," Red Mack suddenly proposed, as if the decision was sudden.   "I'll give you fifty dollars for it as it stands."

But the offer seemed to bring the spirit of bargaining to the men.

"I guess we ought to get a hundred, at least," Amos retorted.

"Perhaps," Red Mack agreed, "but not from me."

"Let's take the fifty," Howard whispered to his friend.

"At least give us seventy-five," the man compromised.

But Red, usually liberal and not the one to stand on a small amount, was obdurate.

"I can't give you more than fifty dollars," he announced decisively. "Glad to help you fix it, however, if you wish. That would be friendly and wouldn't cost you anything."

"Well, if that's the case, take it for the fifty dollars and welcome. Although, stranger, it's no kind return for your friendliness, to take your money and saddle you with this car."

"But, I'm used to mules and all kinds of balky things, including Fords," Red replied laughingly.

"Ted," he added, "you take our friends down to the station on these horses. Leave the horses with Pop and Arthur and come back here on your own. I may need you."

"That's very kind of you, friends; we almost feel guilty in taking your money," 'Amos replied.

But Red and Ted laughed and such was the

RED WAS ALREADY TINKERING WITH THE CAR

contagion of their laughter—the two men joined in.

"So long, friend. Hope we see you again, and that you'll still feel as friendly and well-disposed."

But Red was already tinkering with the machine. He was skilled in the ways of all cars. There was only one thing he loved more —horses. It was an easy matter to fix the engine. The trouble was in starting. He skillfully adjusted the carburetor. When Ted came back, Mack was ready to start the Ford.

"Well, Ted," he said, crank in hand, "this is some find. Our Henry is going to be the most valuable member of the family. We shall nurse it, give it kind words; in return it shall do much work and do it well."

"My," the boy said. "To think of only paying fifty dollars."

"Yes, I would have paid two hundred. It's just the thing we need. Besides, when I get some of these wires fired the self-starter will also be working."

"Do you know, Red, I thought they would refuse. I'd have given them the hundred."

"What for? They would have given it away. Did you tell Pop about it?" Red asked.

"No, he wasn't there. Nor was Arthur. A man was unloading and he told me that they had gone down the road a bit, to see the station master who had gone home."

"I hope they'll see us as we drive up in state. Ready?" he called.

The boy urged his horse forward, but the Ford soon left him behind as Mack threw it on high and gave it enough gasoline to go thirty-five miles.

As he neared the station, however, he slowed up until Ted joined him. The two made their way to the station. As the car chugged along, Ted's father and Arthur who had returned, looked up to see who the newcomers were.

The boy and Red laughed aloud at the look of surprise on the two faces.

"What do you think of our car?" Ted asked.

"Ours?" Arthur ejaculated.

"Ours—bought outright," Mack confirmed.

"Have you any money left?" Jim Marsh asked seriously.

"As long as you felt so inclined to buy, why didn't you get a car? This is an exceedingly venerable Henry, I wot," said Arthur.

"Well, it's ours," replied Red, "so listen to the story."

And he told them of the purchase.

CHAPTER V

TROUBLE WITH MEXICANS

MANY a day after that, when the party of four had to toil and carry, and drag the mine, the old Ford served them well. Many a day they had occasion to bless the forethought of Red Mack in the purchase of the same. Ted became proficient in its handling and made himself useful in more ways than one.

The days flew quickly. Although the work was heavy Ted enjoyed the open life, the hard work. Under Mack's tutelage, he became an expert shot and the occasional game, not very plentiful in the region thereabouts, which fell as trophies to his weapon, was welcome to the camp.

Visitors were rare. Most of these were Mexicans. The camp was twenty miles from the nearest village and almost inaccessible, as the roads were bad. Those Mexicans who did come stayed but a little while.

Red Mack had advised a policy of aloofness, so that visitors would not be encouraged to come again and none of these visitors from across the border were permitted to feel at home.

The mine from the very first gave promise, but it was the kind of promise that meant but small returns.

"The thing to do is to keep pegging away. At least our efforts are not fruitless." It was the older Marsh who spoke.

"And success may come any day," Arthur hopefully added.

"It's better for our peace of mind, to think of it as coming this year or next year instead of any day," Red Mack interrupted. "It's slow work at best," he added.

"By the way, Ted," he continued, changing the subject, "better figure on going to the village this morning. We will be needing supplies and there may be some mail."

"From whom?" asked the boy with a knowing smile.

But Red Mack evaded, or rather he did not seem to hear the question. He was sensitive on the subject of Helen, Ted's sister. The two had become great friends and it was Red Mack's hope that it would eventuate in something stronger.

A little later in the morning Ted was off. He reached the village in two hours. His purchases were soon made. There were letters and newspapers for them all.

The news Ted found in the newspapers, which he opened while waiting for his supplies, was extremely disconcerting.

There were big headlines announcing the raid by Villa, the Mexican outlaw, on the little town of Columbus in New Mexico.

The President of the United States had ordered troops to the Mexican border, and the governors of the border states had called out the militia.

"I wonder if it is going to make trouble for us," thought Ted.

There was need to wonder and to worry, too. Columbus itself was a matter of a little over two hundred miles or so from the chain of mountains known as the Perillas in which their camp was located. The Mexican border was very close, the northern boundary of the State of Sonora being but a little more than ten miles away.

"It means war, all right, I guess. We'll have to forget our mining for the time being."

But the boy was given no time in the next half hour for further reflection for the stretch ahead was a hard one and a steady climb.

Then, as he turned at a certain point, he saw two men ahead. A little uncertain as to the wisdom of doing so, he stopped to give them a lift.

The two men proved to be Mexicans. They were singularly forbidding in their aspect and the wheedling attempt of one of them to appear gracious and agreeable made a scar on his left cheek turn livid and almost green.

Not a whit scared and yet exceedingly watchful, Ted drove the car on. The two men behind him, he realized, had all the advantage.

"You belong to the mine up there, boy?" the man with the scar asked.

The boy nodded.

"How many men are there?" the Mexican further questioned.

"Four," Ted replied. He felt it wiser to tell them what they could easily find out for themselves.

The two disreputables conversed between themselves. Ted made out the name of Villa. The Mexican general's name came often into their conversation. From the one or two words he could understand, he gathered the fact that they must have been discussing the raid.

Then a sudden idea came to him.

"Perhaps," he thought with misgiving, "they are figuring on other raids."

Ted noticed with increasing interest and some worriment that the two suddenly began jabbering excitedly. Then they seemed to have come to a decision.

And at that moment Ted came to the turn of the road which led to camp.

"I let you off here," he said to the two men who, however, made no movement to indicate their intention of leaving.

"You drive on, instead," the Mexican replied. Two wicked looking guns pointed at him. "Over this way," the man added and pointed down the road—the road to Mexico.

A moment's thinking and Ted decided that it was wisdom to comply for the time being. Escape might be opportune later; at the present moment it seemed as if it could hardly be made.

CHAPTER VI

TED MAKES HIS ESCAPE

"WHAT do you want?" the boy asked, after he had gone ten miles and the car was nearing Mexico.

"Want?" the Mexican replied. ""Why, we want you to take us to Mexico. There are good reasons for our leaving the States," and the man laughed grimly. His partner, who did not seem to be able to talk English but who understood somewhat, laughed with him.

"Well, we'll soon be there," the boy replied. "Can I go back then?"

"Maybe," the man offered. But he said it in such a way that it made the boy doubt whether he would be allowed his freedom.

His active mind began to speculate on escape.

"About this time," the boy thought, "father and Red will begin to think I should be back. In about an hour they will start on a hunt.

"Luckily, these tires are leaving a trail that they can't help but follow. But what good will it do, if I am already in Mexico when they catch up with it?"

The thing to do, he decided, was to keep the car on American soil. To do that, the old Ford would have to get balky, to refuse to move. And the Ford, because for once there was a desire for it to give trouble, never went more smoothly.

It was less than five miles now to the border. The road to the town of Douglas branched off here but the two captors did not permit Ted to get off the straight road.

Suddenly the car came to a slow stop.

The Mexican motioned threateningly.

"Can't help it, my friends. Trouble, and I don't know what it is."

While Ted got out of the car to investigate, the two men kept their seats.

"Better hurry with it, boy," the Mexican

warned him. "No tricks. What's the trouble?" he added, suspiciously.

"Something seems to be the matter with the engine," Ted replied, "know anything about a car?" he added.

The Mexican got out to help. Ted was quickly aware of the fact that the man's acquaintance with cars was no greater than his own, which was at best but elementary.

While Ted pretended to tinker with the car the two desperadoes were evidently deciding on a plan. One of them, he who did none of the talking, started off on foot and the other kept a watchful eye on the boy, his gun at a convenient angle.

"You young rascal, I believe you're fooling us. Santos has just gone for some of our friends. If your people catch up with us, it will be but for a little while. We shall make short work of the lot of you."

"We want your mine, we want this car and we think a good gringo is a dead one, so let your friends come."

The boy said nothing.

"Well," he thought to himself, "at least, it will take a lot of Mexicans to get us."

"I wonder," he further speculated, "how long it will take that Mexican to bring help. Mack should be on the way very soon, if not already."

The Mexican grew less watchful. After all, it was but a boy he had to deal with, a boy who did not even know how to repair his car, for Ted's efforts appeared genuine.

Ted's sharp eye did not fail to note the decreasing watchfulness. The car, he felt certain, was ready to continue. Now to make sure, so that his dash to escape should not prove a fizzle. Suddenly he decided on what to do.

"I guess I have it fixed. Shall we go on?"

The Mexican was surprised. However, after a second's thought, he decided since it was in the direction from which his friends would be coming, to let the boy go on.

The car, however, went but a little way before it stopped again. Ted threw up his hands in pretended disgust.

"Have you got the gasoline?" the Mexican inquired.

Ted pretended that this was a new idea and looked to see. As a matter of fact, he knew that he had gasoline in plenty. After taking five minutes of investigation he informed the man that the gasoline was sufficient.

Then the boy got on the seat again. He pretended to try to start. The Mexican watched his fruitless attempts; then he got out of the car—it did not seem as if the boy could make it go.

Now, if ever, was Ted's opportunity. But he waited until the man was off guard.

He tried once or twice again with no results. Then, all ready, with his foot on the clutch, he suddenly released it and shot off.

The desperado made a wild grab at the car. The sudden impetus overturned him and he sprawled on the ground.

Ted made way rapidly while the Mexican unloaded his gun in a vain attempt to stop him.

Two miles down and the boy saw a cloud of dust. A nearer approach proved the party to be his father and the two other men.

CHAPTER VII

More Trouble

TED breathlessly told his experience. He showed the newspapers in which the fear of further raids on the border was mentioned.

Red Mack's mind worked like a flash.

"Red," the boy confirmed his thoughts, "I think they will attack us. They know of the mine," and he further recounted the Mexican's threats.

"We'll go back to the camp," Mack decided. "We have better protection there. Pop, you take the car, go a quarter mile down the road. Stay within hearing of probable gunshot. When you hear rifle shots be off to Douglas and get help. We'll be able to hold them off until it comes. Make the old car go. But remember, we do not want to be sending for help if there is no need for it, so be sure not to go until you hear our shots. Go north and then turn at the fork. It's a little longer but you will be sure to avoid the approaching greasers.

"Be sure you hear our signal," Mack further warned. "We don't want to make a false call and be in the position of the boy who kept shouting 'Wolf, Wolf'."

"I'll be sure before I go ahead," Pop agreed.

Mack, Arthur and Ted repaired to the camp and quickly made a formidable barricade. The big hole which was the entrance to the mine served them as a trench.

They kept a careful watch. Two hours later they were aware of the approach of a number of men. It took but a few minutes to decide the identity of the newcomers.

Mack and Ted took careful aim at the nearest of the Mexicans. Their shots told. They could picture the older Marsh making his dash to Douglas upon hearing the signal.

At his station, Bill Marsh made doubly sure and waited until he heard further shots. Then he was off.

As nearly as they could count, the Mexicans

seemed to number twenty. The three made every shot tell and the outlaws after the first mad charge, in which they lost three men in addition to the first two, who had been wounded, withdrew to cover.

From this position, the Mexicans took occasional shots at the slightest exposure on the part of any of the besieged. Two or three of them, it was apparent, were making a hunt for the Ford—and the failure to discover it must have given them some food for thought.

A lull of more than twenty minutes followed during which the Mexicans evidently were deciding on a mode of procedure. Suddenly the quiet was interrupted by a mad dash from all sides.

Ted was able to protect the rear from his location, the mine making an ideal trench. Arthur and Mack used their guns to equally good advantage.

Two of the Mexicans managed to reach the mine and they vaulted in. It was a reckless, daredevil thing to do, for Red Mack, the very incarnation of power, curiously unlike his usual calm and collected self, disposed of them with the butt end of his pistol. It was hot

THE MEXICAN APPEARED, WAVING
A WHITE SHEET

work; it needed all the agility and sureness of aim of those inside to keep the invaders off.

The desperadoes withdrew to cover. A little later one of them appeared with a white sheet.

Red Mack stood up, the other two covering the Mexican with their guns to avoid treachery.

"You gringoes," it was Ted's acquaintance of the automobile, "had better leave peaceably. More of our men are coming soon—and if you leave now, we will do you no harm. We want your supplies; we want your money and the automobile. We will let you go, however. Afterwards, it will be too late."

"How do we know you will let us go free?" Red Mack inquired, more to carry on the parley, than for any other purpose.

"We shall let three of our men go with you and they will be unarmed. Once you feel safe, you will let these men go free."

"We have very little money and the automobile is not here, otherwise, perhaps, we would consider your offer. But I warn you," Mack continued, "you will pay dearly for this.

It is United States territory and Uncle Sam will punish this."

The Mexican laughed. "Our general is strong and mighty and the gringoes' blood freezes at the name of Villa. Soon he will take away this land which belongs to Mexico and he will punish the dollar-loving gringo. Soon, very soon. Columbus is just a beginning."

"And the end, too," Red Mack replied. "No, we'll stay here. You and your men would be wise to leave now; afterwards it may be too late, as you say."

The Mexican withdrew. What they intended to gain by besieging the camp, the men within could not guess.

"Unless their threat of reinforcement is true," Arthur was now speaking, "if the Mexicans are planning another raid in force at this point."

"Villa must be out of his senses, for to lose America's friendship means his doom, if not at once, in the near future."

"They certainly hate us, don't they?" Ted inquired.

"They're a treacherous lot at best," Mack replied. "They have some reason for their hatred but mostly it's the hatred of the mean and contemptible."

"Wonder how soon 'Pop' will be here with help?" Arthur said.

"Hope he'll be here before sundown. Lucky thing for us the night comes so late at this time of the year."

The sun was already beginning to sink behind the western mountains, a golden ball that spoke the end of a hot day.

In the meantime Pop Marsh had arrived at Douglas. Thirty men, among them a number of Rangers, were quick to answer his summons.

Paced by the car, the horses made fast time, yet, fast as they went, Pop realized it was a race with the night. He knew the need of arriving before darkness came on.

CHAPTER VIII

A Change of Plans

THE desultory firing of the Mexicans, now reduced to twelve, quickened sharply in answer to the volley of the attacking force, which they had espied almost at once.

Their attempt to retreat, however, was checked. The thirty men, under the leadership of Walter Payne, a ranger, encircled them. The outlaws made a wild dash for safety but not one of them got through the net.

Red Mack emerged from his protection.

Payne turned to him. Surprise and recognition showed on both faces.

"Hello, Wally," Red Mack greeted him.

"Hello, Red. You're a sight for sore eyes. As a matter of fact, though, if we knew you were among this group, we wouldn't have wor-

ried.   Gentlemen," and Payne turned to the
thirty odd men, "this is Red Mack, young in
years but an old timer, and true blue."

Another man among the group who talked
Spanish fluently—questioned the Mexicans,
but all of them refused to volunteer information.   This, he expected, but Oliver, the questioner, noticed that one of the Mexicans seemed
to hesitate—showed less of the stubborness of
the other worthies.

The opportunity came a little later and he
and Payne together with Ted and Mack
managed it so that the Mexican was alone
with them.

Oliver's surmise was correct. The man, after a little urging and upon the positive promise of secrecy and protection, divulged the plan
of the Mexican outlaws, under Villa, to make
raids along the whole border. One had been
planned at Douglas, to take place the next day
and other men in addition to the present group
of Mexicans, captured by the Americans, were
to make their invasion from the north. For
that reason, it was Villa's intention to have
this group enter the United States at this
point west of Douglas and circle around so as

to attack the town simultaneously with the coming of the men direct from Mexico. The prisoner gave the location, the points of attack as he understood them.

After obtaining all this information, Payne turned to Red Mack. The latter had explained about the mine and their hopes to his friend.

"I'm afraid you'll have to give it up for the time being," Payne advised. "There's going to be trouble with these greasers and there is almost no way of keeping them off unless we have a large force stationed hereabout.

The four partners looked at each other. Yet not one of them but was ready to meet the fortunes of war unflinchingly. Let it come, if it had to!

"Well, we'll have to talk it over," Red Mack answered. "It may have to be."

The men returned to Douglas, with the prisoners. Payne, however, stayed behind. He was glad to be with his friend, and Red Mack in addition was glad to have him with them in case of trouble.

Ted liked Payne—and the latter as he

crushed the boy's hand in a cordial hand-shake, grinned in friendly fashion.

"So, you've been helping to keep these Mexicans off too?" he said. Ted, flushing, found himself unable to make answer.

"Well, it's fellows like you who soon make good rangers and soldiers."

Marsh was for closing the camp temporarily and although Arthur was in favor of continuing despite the great dangers, Red agreed with the older Marsh. So did Ted.

Not one of these men was afraid of any accusation of cowardice and therefore they dared to suggest that discretion was the better part of valor. When fighting had to be done there was none readier to respond.

CHAPTER IX

BREAKING UP CAMP

WORK was at a standstill the next day. Payne stayed with them. There was a reason for his staying and it hinged on the decision the partners made as to continuing on or shutting down temporarily.

It was the older Marsh who was speaking.

"It's best to close down. We can transfer all our equipment to safety; we can turn our proceeds into cash and when the time comes, open the mine again without much loss."

"Yes," added Red Mack. "Otherwise we stand a chance of losing all, a chance we cannot take. I agree with Pop."

Arthur said nothing, and having ventured his opinion felt no call to volunteer or offer further advice.

Ted felt that the question was being well taken care of so he merely listened.

There was a pause which Arthur finally broke.

"All right, I guess the decision of the majority is best. But what will we do? I, for one, don't care to remain idle, nor do I care to go back to Canada."

"I have it," Red Mack suggested. "Let Pop take the proceeds home with him and bank it. Ted can go with him, too," he added after a pause in which he seemed to be debating the advisability of another suggestion.

"You and I, Arthur, will stay here. If trouble comes—well, you know, it's our middle name, at times."

"That's what I was waiting for," briskly commented Payne. "I have a suggestion on top of that."

No one had noticed Ted's dejection upon hearing Red Mack's decision.

He interrupted Payne's further discourse.

"Whatever your suggestion, Mr. Payne," he said, "you must count me in on it. I came down for whatever might come, and I don't intend to be sent home," he said with such an air of finality and decision that the men laughed.

"I'm not so sure I want to go, either," added his father.

"Well, one of us must go, of course; by all reason you are that one," Red Mack answered. "I thought Ted would not be amenable to reason," he added with a grin. "And I guess we'll have to have him with us. It's decided that Pop goes home and that the rest of us are open to any suggestion of Payne's—especially if it happens to be a good one."

"Well, my idea is this. We are organizing 200 rangers. It is our purpose to go after the Mexicans, even if we have to go into Mexico to do it. We intend to put the fear of the Lord and of Uncle Sam into them.

"There was a time when an Americano was respected by a greaser; we intend to have the Mexicans re-obtain that respect."

"How about you?" he asked. "I don't know what we would do with Ted, but you two would be splendid additions."

Arthur looked at Red Mack who was observing Ted.

"Well, very frankly, I don't know what we'll do with Ted," he responded.

"You needn't wonder at all," replied Ted. "I can be of use to the rangers. I promise I won't make any trouble."

"What do you say, Pop?" Red Mack turned to Ted's father.

"The boy can stay if he wants to," the father replied. "I realize there is danger and yet not much more than there has been here. Ted has a natural aptitude for landing on both feet."

"Yes, and the things he'll learn will help to make him the right kind of man." It was Payne who came out on the side of Ted.

Ted glanced gratefully at him but not for more than a second. After all, he felt that the decision was with Red Mack.

The latter was not convinced, however. In his mind's eye he saw a picture of Ted hurt and the necessity of facing Helen, Ted's sister, and the mother, too, with explanations.

"I'm probably more inclined than any of

you to have the boy," he said, "but someone has to think of the danger. We sometimes forget that Ted's a mere lad."

Then as the boy's dejection became evident, he continued:

"But let him come. Only remember, I wasn't the one who was keen about his staying."

"Trust Ted to do his share and do it well and safely," said Arthur.

"When do you think you want to leave, Pop?" Mack asked.

"I guess it will take several days to clean up and store our equipment. I should say by next Tuesday. That gives us five days."

"Good," said Payne. "I'll stick around and help you. But I shall have to go down to Douglas for a day to make final arrangements and get the last news. I'll be back tomorrow afternoon."

The party set to work at once, Payne departing within the next ten minutes.

CHAPTER X

THE RANGERS TO THE RESCUE

IN the meantime and during the month following, events were rapidly keeping pace with the nimble steps of history.

The President had ordered troops to the border. In addition the governors of the border states had taken every precaution to safeguard those Americans on the line. The rangers made a formidable body and the marauders and bandits of the southern republic had reason to stand in fear of the grim and silent men who policed the zone of danger.

Word had gone forth to follow Villa, to take him dead or alive. Despite the protests of the provisional president, Colonel Pershing, who was under the immediate command of General

Funston, (Fighting Fred) had already started in hot pursuit.

Villa's start was a big one. There was little chance of effecting his capture. The wily Mexican would hardly risk combat with the Americans. The mountain fastnesses and approaches were his haven and he quickly took advantage of them.

Ted had made himself extremely useful to the band of rangers. The men of Arizona were doing good work, and although they made no reports—there were many invasions into the Mexican State of Sonora in pursuit of the cutthroats who were out for murder and robbery.

General Funston's line attempted to cover the entire border, but because of the length of the latter such assistance as the rangers gave was extremely valuable.

Red Mack, who was known to many of the rangers, was made assistant to Payne. Ted acted as dispatch bearer. The rangers had requisitioned the Ford which Mack had purchased, paying him the fifty dollars and the cost for the tires he had found it necessary to

IT WAS STILL DAYLIGHT WHEN TED RODE
INTO THE TOWN

purchase. Mack could have obtained more money for the car but there was no desire to take advantage of the state whose guests they were.

It was one afternoon that a rider rode into the camp post haste. He was covered with dust, and he presented a figure weary unto death.

To Payne, who questioned him, he reported that a ranch with twenty Americans had been attacked by a party of about 500 Mexicans. They were holding the attackers off, but help was needed. He had ridden hard, because time was so much an object.

Payne and Mack consulted.

"I guess we'll have to send for extra help," the former said. "Five hundred Mexicans usually means that there are more somewhere about.

"Right you are," Red replied. "We'll start and let Ted go for help."

Ted, glad of the commission, was off at once. Almost immediately after, the rangers galloped away at breakneck speed. They intended to make the thirty miles in record time.

The distance to Naco was more than forty miles. It was there that Ted would find both rangers and troops.

Ted took a horse instead of the car. A short cut to Naco was possible only for man and beast and the beast had to be extremely sure-footed. More than that, Ted knew that it was only in this way that he could join with rangers or troops, as the case might be, when that body of men was detailed to start in aid of the rangers under Payne.

It was still daylight when the boy reached Naco. Hard driving it had been, but he knew without having been told, the great need for assistance.

He found the rangers camped near the town and a body of troops a little further away, Major Baker in command.

To the captain of rangers, Ted made his report at the same time handing him a note that Payne had sent along. The captain advised him to make his report to the major also.

Ted found the latter in a room of a house located near by. The major looked up as Ted entered and the boy saluted.

**A RIDER RODE INTO CAMP, WEARY
UNTO DEATH**

The officer saluted in return.

"A boy scout, eh?" he remarked with a friendly smile.

"Yes, sir," and without any further ado, he plunged into the reason for his call.

"Captain Payne of the rangers has sent me to report that he is in pursuit of the Mexicans attacking a party of twenty Americans. The Mexicans seem to number about five hundred and perhaps more."

"How many men has Captain Payne?" the major inquired.

"Two hundred," answered Ted.

The major rang a bell and an orderly entering saluted.

"My compliments to Captain Roberts of the rangers. Ask him how many men he could send to the support of Captain Payne."

The orderly returned within five minutes. Captain Roberts followed closely.

The two officers greeted each other.

"I think I can send one hundred men to

Payne's assistance," he made reply to the major's inquiry. "That should be sufficient, don't you think?"

"It should. In the meantime I shall wire El Paso to my chief for orders. Can your men start at once?"

Captain Robert's answer was in the affirmative.

He selected a hundred men, immediately upon his return to his own camp and assumed command in person.

"I'm going with you, captain," Ted remarked as the officer made inquiry as to the route.

"Pretty young, aren't you?"

"Yes, sir, but I belong to Captain Payne's command."

"Is that so? Then we surely must have you with us."

The captain called a halt at the headquarters of Major Baker for final arrangements.

"I'll follow, if I get permission. Perhaps it

will mean an encounter with these devils, a possibility devoutly wished for. Wish you good luck, Roberts, and here's hoping we get a share of the fun."

"Fun?" Roberts ejaculated in disgust. "It's Payne who'll have the fun. Chances are he'll clean up the lot before we get there. But thank you for your good wishes."

CHAPTER XI

The Attack

WE will return to Captain Payne's rangers on their march into Mexico.

"It may go hard with us if Ted doesn't get to Naco," Payne remarked as the cavalcade made their way surely and swiftly into the fastnesses of Sonora.

They made a fine sight. Two hundred clean cut, typically American Westerners, each one a born leader and yet proud to be under the command of one who was selected because of special resourcefulness, ability and courage.

Clear-eyed men, men who would withstand all the vicissitudes that fate and fortune might bring, and each one by his act of gladly accepting the leadership of one of their number, giving the best proof of his greatness.

They welcomed the probability of action,

the possibility of clashing with the hated greasers. A joyous body, yet a silent one, for the work ahead would be done best with the absence of noise and excitement.

Red Mack laughed. "If Roberts is at Naco, it is safe to count on Ted's delivering your message to him." And then as they rode on he told of some of the things the boy had done, just who he was.

Captain Payne was clearly impressed.

"He's such an unassuming lad," he remarked. "What he has done, hasn't spoiled him at all, has it?"

"He isn't the spoilable kind," answered Ted's friend. "Many boys would have had a case of swelled head, but this boy listens, he respects the opinions of older people. He'll prove very useful to us, you can rest assured."

"It isn't that I fear the number of the Mexicans. It's that more may come to their aid. And do you know, Red, an attempt like this is all right if we should prove successful. But, someone will have to be the scapegoat in case it should turn out disastrously. Absence of orders, etc., and Wally Payne may be very severely brought to task."

Red Mack looked back at the men.

"It would have to be quite a number to beat us," he remarked speculatively.

"Those greasers have learned to fight," answered Payne. "Make no mistake as to that."

They made a sharp turn here and Captain Payne marked the trail in a way peculiar to the Rangers. It was similar somewhat to the blazed trail of the scouts.

They covered another ten miles.

"How much further, Jackson?" Red Mack inquired.

"Another twenty minutes," the guide replied. Ten minutes later Captain Payne called a halt.

He arranged his men. It was his intention to make the attack sudden. Even as these final preparations were completed, one of the men observed rising smoke.

"They have fired the house," Jackson excidedly advised them.

"Ready men? Quiet everybody. Don't shoot until we're on them."

Swift as the wind, the men rushed forward to the attack.

Shouts met them, excitement and scampering. The Mexicans, unprepared for the attack at first gave way, but only in the first few moments of the surprise. In remarkably quick time they reformed and met the onrush of the Americans.

The attackers were the surer shots, but the Mexicans vastly outnumbered them. And though many of the Mexicans fell, there were any number to take their place.

Payne gave a sharp order and his men gathered for a temporary retreat. The Arizonas retired about a hundred yards and there they took advantage of the natural protection of a hillock.

"We'll have to try this for a while," Payne remarked. "Will you, Arthur, and you, Lutz, reconnoiter and see what and how strong the enemy is?"

The two men, on foot, made off. They managed to near the enemy's camp from the south. As they watched and estimated the number of the Mexicans, Arthur noticed two of them make off on foot. They were coming their way. He pointed them out to his partner and nodded his head.

Arthur and Lutz crawled into the further depths of the woods. In a few minutes they heard the two Mexicans crashing forward. As they closed on them, Arthur and Lutz arose. The outlaws made as if to shout but the threatening guns in the hands of Lutz silenced them. Arthur also with gun in hand, motioned for the men to follow.

The men hesitated, uncertain, but only for a second for Lutz cocked his pistol. He meant business and they realized it.

"Bien, bien," one of them whined. They started off. When the two Americans brought them to Captain Payne, the latter directed one of his men who knew Spanish to question them. But the prisoners proved stubborn and would give no information.

"My own opinion," said the interpretor, "is that they were off for re-inforcement."

"That must have been it," agreed Red Mack.

"Well, if that's the case, our friends over there will have a trifling longer wait than they anticipate.

"Here they come," suddenly called one of the watchers on post.

"Good," said Payne, "that's what we want. A few such attacks by them and it will leave our numbers a little more even.

The Americans held their fire until the attackers were close upon them.

A veritable blaze greeted the rushing horde. Men fell in numbers and such was the force of the volley that the Mexicans retired, confused, almost in panic.

"Now men, at them," Payne called, and the attacked became attackers in turn. But, they had to retire in short order. The Mexicans numbered more nearly a thousand than five hundred.

The men in the house had evidently devoted their entire time to putting out the fire. In this they seemed to have been successful. Suddenly they raised a flag—the Stars and Stripes.

"Good old flag," remarked **Red Mack**.

The men cheered—it was an inspiring sight.

"If help doesn't come to the greasers, we can easily keep them off until Roberts' men appear. They'll be due in two hours."

One of the men now noticed two moving bodies crawling toward their line.

"Halt," he called, "who goes there?"

The two bodies stood up and made a wild dash toward the rangers.

"Why, they're boys," Red Mack remarked in astonishment.

The breathless lads, safe among friends, turned grinning, friendly faces to the men.

"Well, lads, who are you and where did you come from?"

"We"—they started to answer, but Jackson forestalled them.

"It's Jerome and Benton. They belong over there," and he pointed to the house.

"How'd you get here, and why?" Captain Payne asked sternly.

"We volunteered. Father wanted to get word to you that a big band of Mexicans was at Bacoachi."

"That's the point to which our prisoners must have been bound," said Payne. "Very well, Benton and Jerome, make yourselves at home."

"Father told us to tell you another thing," Benton added. "He said, if any of you wanted to get to the house to fire twice and they would be on the watch."

Captain Payne nodded understandingly and Red Mack took the boys under his wing. He had a strong admiration and liking for all boys who seemed as self-reliant and frank and open as did these two lads.

CHAPTER XII

TED BRINGS HELP

CAPTAIN ROBERTS and his small number of men rode fast. Ted, glad to have been allowed to come along, kept his place in the forefront. He was a good rider and his horse was swift and sure-footed.

In due time they came upon the tracks of Payne and his men. After that it was an easy matter to follow the course taken by the first body of men.

But it was several hours and late in the night when they neared the scene of hostilities.

At a point which Captain Roberts thought must be near their quest, he called a halt. He deployed several of the men to scout the location on all sides.

Within ten minutes, two of them had returned. The Mexicans were immediately ahead, they reported. In less than twenty minutes all the scouts had returned, the last man bringing Red Mack with him.

Captain Roberts and Red were old friends. The two went into conference at once.

"My idea," said the former, "is to keep our position here until the first rays of morning. At exactly four o'clock we both will attack, front and rear. What do you say?"

Red Mack told him how many the Mexicans numbered.

"It seems to me," he said, "our attack should be now. At any moment they may get help in large numbers.

"It occurred to me that we could perhaps obtain some lamps fed by calcium carbide, perhaps acetyline, at the big house. Most likely they would have it."

"Wonder how we could get to the house?" Roberts pondered.

Red Mack suddenly bethought himself of the information Jerome and Benton had brought. He told this information to Roberts.

"We had best send some one to find out. They could get the lamps ready and then we could obtain whatever they have and divide them equally," said the captain.

"If the lamps do nothing else it will show our mutual positions and so we can avoid attacking each other," Red volunteered.

"Also show us to the enemy," was Robert's pessimistic rejoinder.

"Our shots will do that, for that matter.

"Let Ted go to the house," he added. "Here, Ted," he called.

Ted came forward. He had been too excited to sleep—although with the exception of four men who were on guard—all the other rangers were fast asleep.

"Go to the house. Find out what they have in the way of lamps that give a strong light. Tell them the position we hold from the house. 'Also that we will call in twenty minutes for these lamps. They already know the position Captain Payne holds."

"It may be," Roberts added, that they have a spot light or some similar contrivance. Many of these big ranches have them. If so, let them play it on the greasers."

Some further instructions followed.

Red Mack fired his gun twice. The men asleep were instantly up and alert. Through the other two camps of armed men, noises were heard, mutterings, then after a while quiet again resumed sway.

Red Mack pointed out the direction of the house, which made a dim and shadowy figure.

Ted crawled forward. He made fair progress. When he reached the house he had to circle it to find the entrance. From his position flat on the ground, he threw a small stone at the house. It made but a slight, a very slight sound, but Ted saw the door open at once.

He managed to get inside.

The entire household observed him with surprise. Those who had been asleep and not on watch had been awakened by the pistol shots and were awaiting the expected visitor. Their astonishment must have been similar to that of Payne's and his men at the sight of Jerome and Benton.

"What have we here?" said Mr. Day, father of the two boys.

Ted briefly explained and announced the news of the reinforcements. He inquired about the lamps.

Day's reply was a great relief.

"We're plentifully supplied with calcium carbide lamps, and the calcium carbide. They are small but there must be twenty to thirty of them. Then we also have the big calcium light which we'll prepare. The small lamps are ready for use at any time."

A little later found six of Roberts' men at the door. Red Mack and three others soon followed.

Red Mack decided that the spotlight should be turned on at the first shot. He told one of Roberts' men that the attack would be begun by Capt. Payne and rifle shots would be the signal.

A half hour later found the fight in full blast. The lights served well, the house light in particular, as it played with full force on the enemy. The attack of Captain Roberts' men was a surprise and it had the desired effect.

The Mexicans retreated. They made but small effort to fight. Thirty of them were captured including one who seemed to be the leader or general.

The first rays of morning found the Mexicans in full retreat and the rangers resting.

"Now," said Captain Payne to Mr. Day, "it's up to you to prepare to return to the States."

"We're ready now," the man replied.

Red Mack had introduced Ted to the two boys who were a little younger. The three had immediately started on a hunt for such guns as the fleeing Mexicans had left behind.

They found but few, however. Mexican arms were too scarce not to be preciously guarded. The loss of arms was almost sufficient cause for imprisonment and worse even though the culprit gave the best of reasons.

In his search Ted suddenly came upon a large envelope in which were some papers. He glanced through them.

"What is it, Ted?" Jerome inquired.

"They're in Spanish," replied the former.

"What are you going to do with them, Ted?" Benton asked, all interest.

"Take them to Mack, he can decide."

Suiting action to words, the three boys found Red Mack and turned the papers over to him. Red Mack called to Captains Payne and Roberts and to Mr. Day. The latter was well versed in Spanish. As he read through the papers, a whistle of amazement escaped.

"These papers should be in General Funston's hands. And quickly, too. They appear to disclose the plans of Villa, what he intends to do. His attack on Columbus and such other attacks as he has planned are to get the United States to intervene and so unite entire Mexico under his leadership."

"Who shall take them to the general?" Captain Payne speculated. But he answered his own question. "How about you, Mack?"

"Sure," replied the latter. "Ted and I will be glad to do it."

"We'll probably go to El Paso ourselves," remarked Mr. Day. "We can travel together."

"What are we going to do with our prisoners?" inquired Captain Roberts.

"Let them go. Theoretically we have no right on this side of the border and the sooner we get away the less we'll hear about it. All that would happen to these prisoners would be that they would be freed or turned over to the Mexican government."

CHAPTER XIII

STOPPING OFF AT COLUMBUS

INSIDE a Pullman the Day party with Red Mack and Ted who had joined it, was on its way to El Paso.

"That certainly was a lucky shave," said Mr. Day, referring to his trouble with the Mexicans. "Now that we are out of it, I must say that things were pretty blue for a while."

"You should have seen Jackson when he came to camp," commented Red Mack. "I don't believe he could have gone another step."

"But, father," interrupted Mrs. Day, "you never told us we were in so much danger." Good Mrs. Day began to worry anew over the things her family had escaped.

"Of course I didn't tell you, my dear. It was enough for me to know. I want to say this for the Rangers: they certainly were quick to respond."

"That's one advantage in having an unofficial force," said Red Mack. "Uncle Sam's soldiers couldn't have entered Mexico. All that could have been done would have been for the President to wire the government in Mexico City."

"A lot of good that would have done us. No, thank you," Mr. Day asserted, "I'm thankful for such a force as the Rangers who go ahead and do things and explain their actions afterwards."

"But suppose we forget about past troubles," he continued. "Have you or Ted ever met the general?"

"No, we have not," Red replied.

"Well, you have something in store for you. He's a plain man and offhand you would never suspect he is the great soldier he is. But the men love him and when Uncle Sam needed a real man on the job down here, he sent Funston."

The talk continued, now changing from conditions in Mexico to the big war and Canada's part in it. Mr. Day had learned that Red Mack and Ted had come from there.

"I can't help feeling that we will get into it," Red Mack remarked.

"We certainly should," said Ted, who had been listening.

Ted's tone, without any intention on his part, had been so earnest and decided that everyone laughed, including Red Mack.

"Of course," said Red Mack teasingly, "you're prejudiced. I guess you're as much Canadian as American."

"I certainly am not. I like Canada, but I'm for America first, last and all the time."

"Good for you, Ted," Mr. Day approved. "It's a great country and well worth your pride."

"The reason I accuse Ted of being half Canadian is because of what he did for Canada about three years ago."

And so in answer to the interested inquiry

of Mr. Day, Red gave an account of Ted's adventure as narrated elsewhere. Ted found it convenient at this time to join Benton and Jerome who were in the observation car.

"Hello, Ted," the two boys shouted and made place for him.

The three watched the rolling country with great interest.

"This train certainly doesn't stop at many places, does it?" Jerome remarked as they whirled past a rather imposing looking station.

"It's an express all right. They call it the Texas Limited," Ted replied. "But it's going to stop at the next down. I know that," Ted added.

"What is it?" Benton inquired.

"It's Hermanas," Ted answered . "I think it stops there for more than fifteen minutes."

"Let's ask dad if we can't get off for a few minutes," Benton suggested. They hastened back to the older people. Benton asked for the permission. "We shall all get off," his father replied.

A little later, the train began to slow down. The brakeman informed them that the stop would be for thirty minutes.

The boys scampered here and three. Ted, having gotten the proper amount of exercise, joined Red Mack and Mr. Day who were in conversation with the station master.

"They're keeping me busy today," the man informed them. "The general is due at Columbus tomorrow and a number of our folks here are going down. Between that and answering that key I haven't found much free time."

"You mean General Funston?" Ted inquired. He was not sure that he had heard correctly.

"General Funston it is," the man replied, and turned to answer a call.

Red Mack looked at Ted who in turn was questioning him with his eyes.

"Reckon we can stop off there, let the general have these papers, and then continue to El Paso," Red Mack declared.

"That means you leave us, doesn't it?" Mr. Day remarked. "I'd stop off too, but I must be in El Paso at as early a moment as possible. You see," he added, "there is a chance for saving something of my property in Mexico."

"Well, we'll see you in a few days, at the latest," Red Mack replied.

CHAPTER XIV

In Search of a Spanish Dictionary

TED looked with great interest on the town which the Mexicans had so daringly invaded. Columbus, of which but one in ten thousand had heard before Villa's raid, was now a national by-word. There could not be more than five hundred people in it, Ted decided.

"Red," the boy announced, "I had an idea it was a much larger place."

"You must not forget, Ted, that although the town is small, it is the trading place for this part of New Mexico. That's what makes a town of this size in a state like this, so much more important than a city ten times its population in states like Illinois or New York. See?"

"I hadn't thought of that," the boy replied.

They soon found that the general was not expected until late the following afternoon.

"We had better go over to the hotel," Red advised.

"I hope we will be able to take a hike," Ted said. "It seems as if I haven't walked for ages."

"Well, we'll take one later," his friend replied. "I want to write some letters and go over these papers you found. I really haven't had a chance before this. Worse luck! they are in Spanish, and for all the good that does me they might just as well be in Greek."

"I wonder," Ted voiced a sudden thought, "whether we couldn't get a Spanish dictionary in the town."

"That's an idea, Ted. Suppose you make a try for it while I get through with my letters."

"To whom are you writing, Mack?" the boy questioned, at the same time making sure that his hand was on the door and that he could make his escape.

"To Jack Dean and to 'Pop'," the man replied off-handedly. But his eyes were searching for a missile.

"Sure that's all?" Ted further questioned with a knowing look. "You won't be writing to Helen, while the writing's good, will you? Sure?" he added.

He was too late to dodge the shoe which came flying toward him.

"You little imp," Mack called to him, "get out or I'll give you a hiding."

Ted got out. He knew just how far he could tease his friend on this subject and he felt that he had gone far enough.

Rubbing his head where the shoe had struck it, he made his way to the general store.

"Got a Spanish dictionary?" he asked the man who came toward him.

"Spanish dictionary?" the man replied. "I didn't know there was such a thing. What would you want *that* for?"

"I have some stuff that's written in Spanish and I want to know what it means."

"Oh," said the storekeeper. "I was wondering what white folks would want with a greaser dictionary. Reckon if you bring it over here, most everybody knows all the Mexican there is any need for knowing."

But that was not the thing Ted wanted and so after a few more words he left the man. None of the other stores could bring to light anything that was satisfactory. One storekeeper had a Spanish book and offered it to Ted with many apologies for having it in his possession.

"Go over to the school," a man advised him. That was the soundest bit of advice he had gotten so far. The boy's search had lasted for more than two hours but he hated to give up his quest until successful.

At the school—it was long after school hours—he saw a man who seemed to be in charge.

"I'm trying to borrow a Spanish dictionary," the boy informed the man.

"Haven't been very successful, have you?" the latter replied with an amused smile. "Folks around here would consider it a disgrace to own one."

"They certainly haven't any use for the Mexicans, have they?" Ted remarked.

"Do you blame them, my boy? There are two things for which we people down here give devout thanks. That we weren't born niggers or greasers. One's as bad as the other."

Ted didn't laugh. The man was too much in earnest. The boy had never understood the attitude of southerners to negroes. That was because he, like most northerners, had never had occasion to literally rub elbows with them. If the boy had, he was too fair minded not to have understood the prejudice and to have felt it, too.

"Folks up north speak of being reasonable, of not being prejudiced. They say that of the nigger, and they say that of the Mexican. I wonder what those people would do if they had these brutes swarming about them everywhere." The man was speaking on a subject that must have meant much to him.

"But speaking of Spanish dictionaries, I reckon I can help you. The school is about the one place that can, hereabouts."

He went into another room and brought out a well worn book and handed it to Ted.

"I'll bring it back when we're through," he said, after giving thanks.

The man, Ted had noticed, had expressed no curiosity as to what use the boy intended to make of the book.

Ted followed his instincts.

"You see," he confided, "we have some Spanish papers we want to decipher." And he then gave an account of how the papers had been found.

"Where are you and your friend stopping?" the man asked.

The boy told him. "Come over and see us. I'm sure that Mr. Mack will also be pleased to meet you."

"I shall," the man replied. "Some time this evening. Perhaps I'll be able to help you."

Ted returned to the hotel. His course lay past the railroad station. As he neared it, he heard a train coming in from the east.   He was in a hurry to get back so he gave but a casual glance at the passengers who were alighting. Subconsciously, he was aware that there were quite a number, but he did not give it much thought for his mind was still on what his new acquaintance had told him.

CHAPTER XV

Looking for an Old "Friend"

"DICTIONARIES must be scarce about here," remarked Red Mack with a grin, "or you must have already taken your hike. Sorry you preferred your own company."

"You are right in both respects," Ted replied as he sank into a chair. "Dictionaries are scarce; in fact we have the only one of its kind; and it took me so long to find it I did as much walking as I have any wish for."

"But you got it and that's something," Red replied. "I heard the train coming in," he added.

"Yes I saw it," the boy answered. "Lots of people got off, too." And then the boy stopped for a full minute. The picture his eye had snapped of the alighting passengers was beginning to develop.

He rubbed his eyes. Surely, he must be fancying the thing he now saw in his mind's eye.

"What is it?" Red Mack, who had noticed Ted's pause, was watching him.

"Of course," Ted thought, "I'm mistaken."

And so he brushed the fancy out of his mind. "Why, nothing, Red. I just happened to think of something foolish, that's all."

"That shouldn't have made you stop," Red replied laughingly.

He was already studying the dictionary and one of the papers. Ted joined him. As the meaning in the paper unfolded itself Red Mack whistled.

"A nice, lively government that," he remarked. "This Mexican was calmly negotiating with Carranza and his men, although he's under Villa."

"He evidently didn't get all he expected," Ted added, as he read what Mack had translated.

The man was trying to get a large sum from the Mexican government for turning over his

command. It struck both our heroes ludricous-
ly that he had insisted on being paid in United
States gold.

"Here's another one," Ted said.

The new paper disclosed the plan as outlined by one of Villa's men to attack the border towns on the American side.

"It won't do much good now," Ted declared.

"But the general will be glad to get it," said
Red Mack.

All the papers were interesting as the two
laboriously deciphered them.

Red Mack had found one which had given
him considerable trouble in making out. It did
not seem to be written by one who was versed
in the language.

As the meaning dawned on him, he called
excitedly to Ted. "Oh, Ted, here's something
that will appeal to you. I don't seem to get the
whole meaning, but it concerns our German
friends."

Ted dropped the paper he was studying and
came over to Red's side. He read the transla-
tion the latter had put down.

"This is the best I can do with it," Mack declared.

And even as the latter had translated it there was evidence of a Teutonic swing to the words. The paper read in part as follows:

"We, our friends, remember always. With our help, the great Mexican general's desire shall bear fruit. A greater Mexico which he shall rule over."

There was more to this effect and throughout it all there were hints and suggestions as to how the Mexicans could help. There were two lines that brought Ted sharply to and these two were the closing ones:

"Soon, to see you I hope—
                "Frederick Schmidt."

"Then I wasn't mistaken," the boy exclaimed. "I really saw him."

"Saw whom?" Red Mack questioned. "Are you crazy?"

"Red," the boy excitedly told his friend. "I wasn't thinking at the time I stopped at the station when the train came in. I just looked at the people but I really didn't see them. But a little while ago it flashed upon me that one of those I saw get off was Schmidt. But I was sure I was just dreaming, so I brushed the thought aside."

"I see," said Red Mack. "And who is Schmidt?"

"He's the man who met me on the train when I went from Wayland to Chicago and tried to find out on just what business I was bound. He was the go-between for the German embassy and the people who were supposed to attack Canada. I guess he must be doing the same work with the Mexicans."

"You are sure you saw Schmidt?" Red Mack questioned.

"Not sure," Ted made answer. "It's just an impression."

"I wonder if he saw you," mused Red. "Still," and he inspected the boy closely, "he'd hardly recognize you, for the two years have changed you considerably."

"Let's take a walk and see if we can't find our German friend," he added.

Ted suddenly bethought himself of the

promised visit of the man he had met at the school. He informed Red Mack of this.

"Well, we have time to eat and also take this walk," was the reply. "We will leave word that we shall be back at eight in case your friend comes before then."

Ted walked over to the clerk. "I expect the school teacher to come up here about eight o'clock," he said. "Will you tell him if he comes before we get back to wait for us?"

The clerk laughed. "The school teacher is no he," he replied. "She's a very nice she. And I reckon my boy, she's not coming up here at eight because company's keeping her busy."

"Who is the man that's staying down at the school house?" the boy asked.

"I admit he stays down there a good deal of the time," the clerk replied, glad to gossip and to volunteer information. "His name's Nixon. I guess he's just visiting. He's the company aforementioned."

"Thank you," the boy said, and joined Red Mack.

They strolled through the town. While Ted had been talking with the clerk his friend had looked over the register. He made certain that Schmidt had not taken a room at the hotel for there was only one name entered and that could hardly have been Schmidt, even under a nom-de-plume, for it read "John Mason and wife." There was of course a chance that Schmidt was Mason but from the style of the writing he felt sure that this was not so.

Ted informed his friend of his mistake in presuming that the man he had met was the school teacher. Red Mack laughed at Ted's description of the clerk's method of putting him right.

Everywhere they went, they found the American flag in plentiful display. This was in celebration of tomorrow's event. There were also a number of Uncle Sam's boys in town. They had come in for the evening from the camp located nearby.

The two entered a small restaurant for their evening meal. This passed without incident. Both Ted and Red Mack had been keeping a sharp watch for any man who would answer the description of Schmidt. The town was so small it was natural to expect that they would run across him during the night. Every one in town came to the main street some time during the evening. But if Schmidt was in town he managed to keep himself out of sight.

"It's time to turn back, Mack."

"What time is it?" Red inquired.

The boy looked at his watch.

"Not much time left for us to get back at eight. We'll have to hurry. It's almost that now."

"Well then, let's do it," Mack replied. "If Schmidt is here, we're sure to run across him later."

A little after eight they entered the hotel.

CHAPTER XVI

The Papers Disappear

NIXON was already there and with him was a very attractive young lady. He stood up as the two came toward him.

"My name is Nixon," he said. "That's something you didn't find out, when you were down at the school house, did you?" he laughed at Ted.

"No, but I've had this information volunteered to me and lots more," Ted replied.

The young lady laughed and blushed. So did Nixon.

"This is Miss Manning," Nixon introduced her. "I presume that this is Mr. Mack, since I heard this young man call you that."

"That's my name," Red replied. He had taken an instant liking to Nixon.

"Now, what's your name, my boy. To think of my loaning so rare a thing as a Spanish-English dictionary to someone whose name I don't even know."

"Perhaps you loaned it so readily, because it wasn't yours, and happened to be mine," Miss Manning suggested.

The laugh that followed made everyone feel at home. Then Ted told his name.

"I suppose you both know who Miss Manning is by now and what my supposed business is down here," said Nixon. "As a matter of fact I am down here on business and pleasure combined," he added with a quizzical look at both Red and Ted. "The ethics of my profession should make me very secretive. But I'm not, in this case. I think I can get some help from both of you."

Ted looked up. He wondered in just what way he and Red could help. The latter quietly studied the speaker.

"I'm in charge of operations down here for the Secret Service. We have some leads which make us believe that the Germans are coming down here to conspire with certain Mexicans to embroil that country in war with us."

Ted glanced at his friend but the latter made no comment.

"The boy here told me of some papers you have. I wondered if I showed you proper credentials if you would let me see those papers. Of course I can get them from General Funston but he may be delayed and if there is any information contained in those papers they may be of value even before he comes. I can satisfy you," he turned to Mack, "as to my identity."

"I hardly need that," the latter replied. "As a matter of form, however, I shall be glad to look at them. Well, Ted?" he turned to his companion. Although he was certain as to how Ted felt, he wanted him to feel that he was also being consulted. Nixon had asked Red the question only because he was the older of the two.

"Show them to him. And tell him of my suspicions," Ted replied.

The four went upstairs to a smaller sitting room. Ted brought out the papers he had found.

It was Miss Manning who quickly deciphered each of them. Her knowledge of

Spanish was thorough. There were some new meanings to some of those that the two had so laboriously translated. But Nixon, it was clear, found most satisfaction in the letter from Schmidt.

"We knew something of this," he said, "and we have been on the watch for him and his companions. Most of this other information is for the general but this is specifically applicable to the case I am working on."

Then Ted told of having seen or rather that he thought he had seen the man Schmidt.

"Do you know him?" Nixon asked. "And how?"

Again Ted had to tell of Schmidt's activities in Chicago and just how it happened that he knew him.

"You should be very useful," Nixon commented gleefully.

"We've tried to locate him but haven't been very successful," Red told him. "It may be that Ted was mistaken. Although I'm ready to admit that the coincidence of coming across his name in this way is remarkable."

"I suppose," Ted said, "the important thing

is to get Schmidt in the act of conspiracy, isn't it?"

"This letter you have here helps," Nixon replied.

The three discussed the question further. Upon Nixon's invitation, Mack and Ted, after first taking the papers to their room, accompanied the latter and Miss Manning to an ice cream parlor. Nixon had kept those papers that concerned the German activities.

It was close to ten o'clock when the two made their way back to the hotel after having arranged an appointment with Nixon for the morning.

In the act of undressing, Ted's eye glanced at the place where they had carelessly placed the papers brought back to the room. He did not see them.

Mack had stepped out of the room and in the meantime the boy, still unsuspicious, looked in the dresser. There was no sign of them.

Now a little quicker in his actions he searched his bag. Then he looked through Red Mack's belongings.

Breathlessly he hurried out to the bathroom to find Red.

The latter, dripping wet, opened the door in answer to the boy's alarmed knock.

"Red," the boy was greatly excited, "did you put those papers away?"

"No," Mack answered. "We brought them back to the room, didn't we?"

"We did," Ted replied, "but now they're gone."

Red Mack took the news quietly. "I'll be with you in a few seconds and we'll make a thorough hunt. In the meantime go to the sitting room and see if they're there."

When Ted came back from his thorough but unsuccessful search Red was already in the room. He was not any more successful in his search than the boy had been.

"They're certainly not here," he said. "Now, let's sit down and do some thinking."

CHAPTER XVII

Our Friend Schmidt

OUR friend Frederick Schmidt was unusual. To say that of any man, is in itself a mark of distinction, but even more could be said of him to prove his ability, his resourcefulness. His personality was not exactly pleasing but he was at all times extremely convincing. He could put his side of the case so clearly, so alluringly, that against your better judgment, even against your desires, you were almost ready to admit he was right.

Ted was correct. It was Schmidt whom he saw. Schmidt, however, had not seen the boy. Had he seen him there remained a question as to whether he would have recognized him, for as Mack had said, the boy's change had been considerable.

Schmidt had come to Columbus for two reasons. One, it was one of the roads to Mexico. He had no fear as to the Americans' stopping him, for thanks to a rather active and thorough organization in Washington, he had all the necessary papers to prove that he was what he wasn't. The Mexicans, he knew, would not interfere with his entrance into Mexico, because they expected him.

Then too, he knew of General Funston's expected arrival in Columbus. He had never seen this man. Word had gone forth from the embassy that here was a man who commanded respect. He was no mean foe. So Schmidt had a great desire to see him at close hand.

Even in so small a point as Columbus, there were friends to be found. Not that these friends had any suspicion as to Schmidt's errand. But because he had German blood he was received; the glad hand of hospitality was extended to him by German-Americans who lived in Columbus.

One of these had met him at the station and had invited him to his house. He had stayed late and therefore was delayed in getting to the hotel. That was why Mack had not found his name in the register when he searched it.

It was Schmidt's intention to journey into Mexico immediately after he had seen the general. There was a thought beginning to shape itself in the man's mind. Things might be so arranged that a man could be found who for the jingle and possession of silver would be glad to kill and to whom it would not matter whether the corpse was a general or anyone else. There were so many Mexicans, he knew, for whom the possibility of possessing money would be sufficient inducement for crime.

The idea was new. He decided to give it further thought somewhat later.

Not more than three minutes had passed between the exit of the party bound for the ice cream parlor and the entrance of Schmidt into the hotel in search of a room.

The clerk twirled the register toward him.

Schmidt's practiced eye took in the names upon that page. That was purely habit and not because of suspicion.

And so the one thing happened that had not occurred to either Red Mack or Ted.

The name of Theodore Marsh was there.

That brought but a dim recollection to the man. He had come across the name. But in a life that was extremely eventful, an incident of two years back was vague.

"Where have I come across that name?" he thought. He was thorough. Suspicions of this kind were not lightly tossed aside.

In the act of putting his name down he paused.

"A pretty busy place, is it not?" he asked.

The friendly clerk told him why.

"I suppose all these people who are stopping here are officers then."

No, they weren't. The clerk described some of them. It was a very easy matter to get the information Schmidt wanted.

"It's that Chicago boy," he recollected after the clerk's brief description.

"May I see the rooms?" he asked.

The clerk looked at his list of vacant rooms. He was inclined to be lazy and so he welcomed the suggestion of the man that he need not trouble to go with him to show the rooms.

"I think it will be easy to find," Schmidt declared.

He had noticed the number of Ted's room. Purely as a matter of precaution he made sure that no one was inside and with almost no trouble opened the door.

He was greatly astonished to discover the papers almost at once. Perhaps he spent more time than was necessary in going over them. Suddenly, he heard talking and the talk was coming toward him.

If Schmidt had had time to think he might have left the papers there. After all, he already knew what was in them and no doubt the people who occupied the room also did.

But he was German. The German, as a rule, needs time to think. The exceptions, of course, only prove the rule. He did not leave the papers. He made his escape through the window with them. Down a rickety fire escape, then onto the floor below, he made his way out into the hall.

He told the clerk he did not wish a room. He had an idea, he said, that the rooms had baths and since they didn't, he must look elsewhere.

And before the clerk could recover his poise over this novel reason for refusing a room, the man had treated him to a cigar and had gone. The cigar was a good one and somehow it took away the fluency of expression from such thoughts as the clerk may have had.

Ted and Red Mack, as you may see, had missed Schmidt by but a few moments.

The latter returned to the people at whose house he had dined and whose invitation to stay the night, he had at first refused. It would have surprised the clerk to know that the room Schmidt now had was not only without a bath but without running water as well.

Schmidt brought out the papers again. Carefully and thoroughly he studied each of them. German efficiency and thoroughness, as you see.

He was through now. He chuckled as a thought entered his mind.

"I'll bet that boy would give a lot to know who took those papers."

That was a bet Schmidt would have lost. He also had made a mistake. It did not occur to him that Ted might know he was in town.

"PLEASE THROW UP YOUR HANDS,
MR. SCHMIDT"

He knew that someone did, however, in the next second. There was a noise at the window. Startled, he turned about.

"Please throw up your hands, Mr. Schmidt," said a very polite voice. "They promise a nice, sunshiny day tomorrow and you may wish to see it. If you do, up go your hands."

Schmidt undecided looked at Red Mack.

"You have the advantage of me, but if it pleases you that my hands should go up, why, I'll put them up. Especially so, since you use so persuasive an argument," and he looked at Red Mack's gun.

Mack vaulted over the window sill before the man could move.

"Those papers, please? Thank you. I hope you're not so sleepy that we cannot take a walk? For that's what I'm planning."

CHAPTER XVIII

RED MACK MOVES

RED MACK and Ted had at once decided that Schmidt in some way had obtained information as to the papers' being in their possession. Just how that knowledge had come to him neither was prepared to say.

"Well, they're gone," Red had declared. "There's nothing we can do tonight as far as I can see, so my vote is for bed. We can get up in the early morning and see what we can do."

Ted had to agree with Red's suggestion. He was dead tired and fell asleep almost at once.

Mack had noticed the boy's weariness and it was for this reason he had suggested bed. As soon as he was assured of the fact that Ted was asleep, he quietly dressed himself and went downstairs.

"Did you ever get sleepless attacks?" he asked our friend, the clerk.

"The kind of attacks I get are the sleepy kind," was the clerk's reply. "Haw! Haw! That's a funny one, ain't it? He asks me 'Do I have sleepless attacks?' and quick as that, I answer him: 'the kind of attacks I get are the sleepy kind.' Haw! Haw! Haw!" And the clerk went off into a gale of laughter. It certainly was a funny one, he decided.

"That's the second funny one tonight," he added. "Man comes in about half an hour ago. Says he wants a room. He goes up. A little later he comes down and says, says he, 'I didn't know the rooms had no baths.' And walks out."

"Why didn't you prove to him how nice the room really was," Mack asked, after agreeing that that also was funny.

"I wasn't with him. He went up alone to see the room. I bet if I was with him he would have taken it."

"I'm sure he would. He certainly must have been a mollycoddle. Did he look like one?" Mack inquired.

"Not specially. He was dressed well, had a fancy mustache and wore glasses. Didn't act much like a dude."

The brief description fitted Schmidt. "I bet he wanted to know all about everybody here? That kind of people are usually very curious, aren't they?"

The clerk agreed. He didn't know why that kind of people should be, but he agreed, nevertheless. "Yes, he was the curious kind."

"Where do the folks about here come from?" Mack inquired. "Are they Texans?"

"They come from everywhere. I'm from Indiana. Some are from Texas. Others from different states. We have greasers and even chinks."

"I thought I saw some foreigners today," said Mack.

"No, no foreigners that I know about," replied the clerk.

"Well, they certainly looked the image of Germans," Mack insisted innocently.

"You must mean either the Timms or the Brodys. But they're not foreigners. They lived down here long before I did," his informant advised Mack. "They're German-Americans. Maybe you saw that man who was here. He looked either like an Englishman or German."

"No. Those people I saw lived down the street. About three squares down, I would say."

The clerk thought it over. "The Timms live in the first house on the second side street. The green house, the big one. The Brodys live a half mile to the north. I can't seem to recall who lives where you say."

"I may have been mistaken," the questioner decided. "Reckon I'll be taking a walk. Maybe, that will make me sleep."

Mack sauntered out. He did not seem to have a purpose in the world. His questioning of the clerk had seemed meaningless, as if intended only for the passing of time.

He realized that quick action was necessary with Schmidt. Otherwise the man would have too much advantage. He hated to find it necessary to tell General Funston that the papers had been stolen,

A light was burning in one of the rooms of the house which the clerk had described as belonging to the Timms. Cautiously he approached the window. He glanced in. He could see a man studying some papers. Mack watched him for ten minutes. He had prepared his plan of action. And as the man moved, so did he. The next few seconds are covered in our previous chapter.

CHAPTER XIX

MACK JOINS THE SECRET SERVICE

"MR. SCHMIDT," remarked Mack conversationally, "when we enter the hotel no one need know who you are. However, that won't change your actual position. If you need any assurance as to my ability to shoot, I can tell you, I hardly ever miss. Of course, you can say that you have only my spoken word for that, but it is for you to decide as to whether that assurance is sufficient. You can have other proof should you wish to take the chance."

"Thank you," replied Mr. Schmidt, who seemed calm and self-possessed. "I shall decide as to that."

"In the meantime, until you decide, my gun will be in my pocket and my hand, too."

"Hello," the clerk greeted them in surprise.

They entered the hotel.

"Our friend has decided he will stay here for part of the evening, although the room will be without bath. This way, Mr. Schmidt."

Schmidt studied Mack coolly for a second. Then he obeyed.

Upon their entrance into the room, Ted woke up. He rubbed his eyes incredulously.

"Good evening, Mr. Schmidt," he said, with a grin. "And all this time I've slept. I'll never forgive you, Red."

"Ted, you find out where Nixon is staying. Tell him to come here as quickly as possible."

In two minutes, Ted was gone. He asked the clerk if he knew where Nixon was stopping. Of course the clerk knew, but he was also curious. Finally he had to be satisfied with the promise of later information.

Ted telephoned. After a long wait, Nixon answered. He promised to come over at once.

Twenty minutes later, the clerk, no longer able to hold his curiosity, ushered in the expected arrival. Much to the clerk's disgust, however, he was not allowed to stay.

"This is Mr. Schmidt," announced Red Mack. "Better have him placed where he will be more comfortable and where he will have less occasion for indecision. He hasn't decided yet as to whether he could get away if he made the try.

"I want to assure you again, Mr. Schmidt, that a sunshiny day even from prison walls is worth while. I really am a very good, a very sure shot. So do not waste your days in repenting over the fact that you did not attempt escape. At least your days are the longer for it."

Nixon, Red Mack and Ted escorted the prisoner to the United States camp. There he was placed in safe custody.

Then Mack gave an account of the capture. Ted looked with great pride at his friend.

"I'm going to ask that you be appointed my assistant," Nixon advised him. "We need you."

With the morning came news that the general, who was not a well man, would not come to Columbus. Instead he had sent Lieutenant Perkins, his aide. This was a great disappointment to the citizens of the town and its visitors. The announcement read that the general would come as soon as his health permitted and when the time offered.

Nixon and the lieutenant were great friends. The lieutenant found it necessary to stay for a few days and in that time, Ted and Mack had occasion to see him often. Ted liked the surroundings at the camp and made himself very useful.

On the last day of the lieutenant's stay, word came of Mack's temporary appointment to the Secret Service.

As the lieutenant, Nixon, and Red Mack were passing along a narrow road that morning, they came upon Ted and a sergeant. The latter was in the midst of showing Ted some of the more intricate points of the drill.

"He isn't bad, is he, sergeant?" asked the lieutenant.

"Bad?" replied Sergeant O'Connor. "Faith, he's better than the best man in my troop."

"Well, then there is nothing left for us to do but to make a young soldier out of him," replied the officer. "How about it, Ted?"

That was the beginning of a long friendship between the officer and the boy. Red's opinion of his young friend helped to make the friendship all the stronger.

When the officer returned to El Paso carrying the papers which Mack had given him, Nixon, Red Mack and Ted went with him. In another part of the train Schmidt, under escort, was also on his way to that city.

CHAPTER XX

TED IS SUMMONED

THE general paced up and down the room. His aide, sitting close by at a desk watched him closely. Acquainted with the general's moods, he knew that his superior was vexed and troubled.

"This is what makes it so hard. Here is Baker who wires of trouble in Sonora. The rangers hasten to help. Can we? No. I have to tell Baker to be watchful, but to keep his hands off. Hold off, hold off, while these slippery Mexicans continue their rapine, murder and what not.

"The worst of it is, it's the only thing to do. There are too many selfish interests which would wish us to enter and subjugate Mexico."

"The Germans are looming large as trouble makers, aren't they?" Perkins questioned.

"That's it. Nothing would satisfy Germany so much as to have the country embroiled with our southern neighbor."

"This prisoner that the young man and boy captured proves that. That was clever work, wasn't it?"

"Have you been able to get any information from Schmidt?" the aide inquired.

"Not yet. But I hope we can. Do you know, Perkins, I like that boy? I always did like the little devils. Know anything of him? Nixon tells me some nice things about him."

"Yes, sir," the aide replied. "Have you heard what he did for Canada and how he happened to know of Schmidt?"

"For Canada?" the general replied. "Tell me."

Lieutenant Perkins recounted the deed of Ted in discovering the plot of the Germans as told to him by Red Mack. The general listened attentively.

"He'll bear watching. Will you send for him? We shall need such boys."

Ted, who had been out with Red Mack, upon his return to the house at which they were stopping, found a notice to appear at headquarters.

Speculating as to the reason, he immediately answered the summons.

He gave his name to the guard on duty in front of the general's office. He was ushered in almost at once.

"You wish to see me?" he said, as he gave the scout's salute. The general observed him from a pair of keen eyes which seemed to read him through.

"Yes," was the reply. "Now sit down. Tell me all about Schmidt, what you know of him, what you have reason to believe he is."

Very briefly Ted told of Schmidt's previous activities as recounted in "Lucky the Boy Scout."

"We have been instructed to keep careful watch of German trouble makers. It seems very much as if war with Germany is but a matter of weeks or months. Men like Schmidt are everywhere. Word came to me only yesterday of German spies who are also trying to make trouble among the negroes and Indians. There is no doubt Schmidt is one of these.

"Now, my boy, what are your plans? I have long wanted a boy of your age to help me as he can in so many ways."

"I am due at the Academy," the boy made answer. "Red Mack and I have just talked over the necessity of my returning."

The general thought for a few minutes.

"We'll arrange it so that you can continue your studies here. I shall find you useful, I am sure, and you will be within reach."

The general was better than his word and quick results followed his action. Red Mack became known to his superiors as one of the keen, watchful men of the Secret Service. It was the kind of work he liked.

Ted continued his school course. He wrote to Syd Graham telling him of the events that had taken place and that his return had been put off indefinitely.

Ted's school work kept him fairly busy. The Mexican situation quieted, but bigger, more troublous, more menacing, came the cloud from across the seas. Thoughtful men realized it was but a question of time before the United States would be embroiled in the Great War. Daily came further proof of the Imperial German Government's treachery.

Yet patiently, Uncle Sam bided his time. Slow to anger, even his patience could not last much longer.

Sad news for the country came at this time; sad news for all who knew the little general, Fighting Fred. He was a man who had made his name illustrious in the Philippines, a man whose worth the whole country realized.

The news of his death was a blow to the country. Ted, who had grown to love him, and who in turn had grown in the general's confidence, was one of the many mourners.

Yet, even so notable an event found its importance but a day's news.

Now the patience of Uncle Sam was at an end. He was quick to act now, as he had been slow to anger. Germany's representative was sent home. Then a few more days, a week, a month and the United States entered the arena.

On the other side of the water, the nations of the Entente breathed a mighty sigh that spoke relief. Already the strain lessened. Encouraged, England, France and Italy girded their armor and prepared once again to conquer the mighty enemy.

CHAPTER XXI

TED AND MACK AT JUAREZ

IF to Syd Graham, the news in Ted Marsh's letter was disappointing, there were two boys who were then making their home in El Paso who were exceedingly pleased with Ted's decision. Jerome and Benton Day had grown to look up to Ted. In their hearts was a great desire to live up to the things he had done.

General Pershing had returned from Mexico. Although unsuccessful in his attempt to capture Villa, he had made such a name for himself as even then gave promise of his immediate greater usefulness.

It was Lieutenant Perkins who acquainted the general with the position Ted had held under the dead chief.

The new officer also had a great fondness for boys, for all children. He took an instant liking to the boy.

School closed early. Red Mack, assigned to duty on the border line, found opportunity to see Ted often.

It was necessary for him to see Lieutenant (now Captain) Perkins one day in reference to some important work. It was a matter that required great secrecy and was of extreme importance. The government had reason to suspect that certain men on the border were German spies. Proof was necessary.

Red Mack asked for Ted, and Captain Perkins immediately assigned the boy to duty. The young soldier had grown used to instant obedience, consequently the duty assigned to him was in line with his desires.

"Now, Ted," Red Mack informed him. "We know there are some officials at the German embassy who are scheming with the German ambassador in Mexico. We know also that other spies are among the negroes. Most of the work is being done at Juarez but occasionally we catch them or get on their tracks when they cross into the States.

"You and I are to go over to Juarez tonight. One of our men who is a Mexican is over there and he thinks he has found one of the haunts of the conspirators."

"But we can't touch them over there, can we?" Ted inquired.

"No, we can't, Ted. But we can perhaps get close enough to observe them. Then, when they do get over here, we can follow them."

Ted nodded his head understandingly.

At sundown, boy and man crossed the bridge to Juarez. Both were dressed in ragged clothing and slouched along to add to their disguise and to act in keeping with their clothing.

When they reached the other side after a second's careless examination by the Mexican customs officials, they were allowed to go on.

A man passed them.

"Buenas noches, senor," he addressed Mack civilly.

"Good evening," Mack replied. "Perhaps I have the honor of addressing Senor Sanchez."

"No, senor," the other answered, "my name is Alvarez."

"Good," replied Mack. "My name is Mack."

This was the agreed conversation as Ted knew. Alvarez briefly narrated where he expected to find the German conspirators.

Mack listened, then inquired: "Have you seen any of them?"

"That is hard, senor. They are extremely cautious, but perhaps tonight we can find out, for I have made arrangements with the owner of the place."

"Good work," replied Mack.

"No, senor, not so good, for I do not know whether I can trust the man. I fear, somehow, he is not to be trusted. But, perhaps, Senor Mack, it is a chance we must take."

"It is worth taking," was the answer, "for we can find out much if things go right. But, do we need this boy?" Mack inquired, anxious not to get Ted into any serious trouble.

"Si, senor. It is the boy who will serve the drinks to the men and who will open the door as he goes in and out so that we can observe. He is but a mere boy and so will not be suspected."

Mack agreed reluctantly. "Very well," he said, "since it must be."

It was close to eight o'clock when Alvarez brought Ted and Red Mack to the small inn. The landlord rubbed his hands and was extremely effusive.

Alvarez handed him some money and the man gave profuse thanks for it. The two men were shown into a small room a door of which led into the big room.

Ted donned a greasy apron. With Mack's and Alvarez' help, he managed to look the part.

"You are dumb, my boy," Alvarez said. "Stupid too, you must be, understand?"

Ted grinned and Mack laughingly remarked:

"It isn't a case of must be. He is."

While the boy got the room in order, one or two Mexicans arrived. Then other men came, some of them Ted guessed to be Germans. They entered into conversation almost at once.

Another man entered. Ted's mind became instantly alert. He recognized him as one of the men had had also been at the conference of the Germans in Chicago, as told in "Lucky The Boy Scout." He did not remember his name but he remembered his face distinctly.

"Hello, Schoen," one of the other men called.

"That was it," Ted mused to himself. "He was the man who had charge of the arrangements for the invasion of Canada."

Another man entered. He seemed to be a man of importance from the greeting given him.

Ted observed each man closely without appearing to do so. He wished to keep a mental picture of each of them before him.

The conversation in the main was in Spanish. Ted wished he could understand. A man spoke to the boy. Ted looked uncomprehendingly at him, then continued at his work.

The landlord bustled in, profusely apologized, and evidently explained the apparent affliction of the boy. He motioned to Ted to follow him. Ted did so.

In a few minutes the boy came back with some bottles. But instead of coming through the general door, he entered by the other door. He carelessly left it open after him. Red Mack glanced through the small opening between the frame and the door. But he could not make out the face of any of the men. He dared not risk taking a better observation.

"At least," he thought, "Ted will get the benefit of a closer view."

Alvarez motioned to Mack, who followed him outside.

"Those two men inside are advising Mexico to make trouble, even to declare war. Germany will help them, so will Japan, they promise. Many Germans in the States will also help."

The American nodded understandingly.

"I think it safest," continued Alvarez, "for us to depart. Either that or take our friend, the landlord, to a place far enough from here to make him safe."

"You still suspect him?" Mack remarked.

"I have been watching him," the Mexican answered. "His mind wasn't made up as to the advisability of which side to play on. I want to save him the trouble of further debate."

"Good," replied Mack. They tiptoed back. But they had hardly resumed their stations when they noticed the landlord motion to the leader of the Mexicans.

"He's made up his mind," Alvarez hissed. "Quick, the lights," he called.

Mack raised his gun and fired at the big lamp. The next instant darkness enveloped the place.

"Out, boy, quick," Mack called, careful not to mention Ted's name.

Pistol shots, noise, confusion. The next second Ted joined them.

"They are over here," the landlord howled.

"This way," he called.

But he was mistaken. The two men and the boy had made a quick get-away and were already on the winding street that led to the bridge.

CHAPTER XXII

German Spies Are Tracked

AS the three slowed up, Ted voiced a thought that had come to his mind.

"Won't they telephone to the bridge station and have us held up on a trumped up charge?"

Red Mack looked at Alvarez. "What chance of that?" he asked.

"It's not only possible but probable. Here," as he swung down a side lane, "we'll go this way."

By a circuitous, roundabout way, the three managed to reach the bank of the Rio Grande, about three miles west of the bridge.

"Now for a boat," the Mexican remarked. "You two wait here. I shall make a try."

He was gone for over an hour. In the

meantime, Ted and Red Mack kept themselves hidden.

"I couldn't get a view of any of the men," Red remarked in a disappointed tone.

"I'm not so sure that I'd recognize the Mexicans but I did study the Germans who were there."

"Think you would know them again?" Mack inquired.

"I'm fairly certain," the boy replied.

"Good, something at least, has been accomplished."

The Mexican returned.

"I found one, finally," he responded to Mack's questioning glance. "It's more than a mile down. I saw some of our German friends," he added, "but luckily our friend the landlord, was not with them."

The boat was waiting for them. The owner was at the oars.

"He is trustworthy," Alvarez assured them.

Once on the other side, the three gave sighs of relief.

"It isn't the possibility of trouble," Mack voiced his feelings. "But, wouldn't we have felt cheap if we had been held over there while the Germans went on with their nefarious business?"

"Well, we may put a nick in their plans," Ted added.

Red Mack immediately reported to his chief.

"You say Ted would recognize the men?" Nixon repeated.

"Yes, he was in the room the entire time."

"I shall ask Perkins to turn him over to the Service for a few days. He may be very useful."

He did this almost at once, calling up Captain Perkins on the telephone the same day.

In the meantime Red Mack informed Ted of what his chief's plans were.

But Ted did not wax enthusiastic.

"What's the trouble?" asked his observant friend.

"Well, there's an officers' corps to train 'somewhere in Texas,' and Captain Perkins wanted me to go there and get such training as I could."

"Of course you will be able to do that, but for a few days—it will take as long as that for the camp to organize—you can work with me."

The objections of Ted were also the objections of Captain Perkins, but Nixon promised to send the boy back within a few days— so the captain reluctantly consented.

Two days later, early in the morning, Red Mack called at Captain Perkins' office.

"I shall need Ted today," he informed the captain.

"Very well, I'll send for him," was the answer.

"We have some work ahead of us," Red advised him. "Come along."

Noon found them on a train bound for Parkerville, a town in Texas. By the old method of eaves-dropping at the ticket office, Red Mack found out the point to which the men were bound. Ted noticed that he went over to a telephone booth immediately after.

"Wonder what they are going out to Parkersville for?" Ted had remarked, as Red Mack came out.

"For no good, that I'll warrant," Red Mack answered. "Ted, you would be surprised at the number of men who are employed by the Germans to foment trouble.

Parkersville was seventy miles from El Paso. They made but slow progress, and it was almost four hours before the train reached the station.

Ted and Mack did not get off when they pulled into the station. Instead they waited until the train had started and then dropped off the opposite side.

It would have been an extremely risky piece of business, if it were not for the fact that the train barely crawled along its course.

They quickly hid behind a freight car which was standing on a siding. From there they observed that a number of negroes had met the men they were watching.

"I think I know what they're after," Red volunteered. "They expect to make trouble among the colored men. They've also tried to incite the negroes in several other places."

"Why?" asked Ted.

"Well, the more trouble we have at home, the less we can help the allies. That's one reason. That's why they are so busily at work in Mexico and even among the Indians. It's all to make trouble."

The watched men walked down the street which led to the main part of the city.

"I wonder how we can find out what they are going to do," Ted inquired of Red Mack.

"Easily enough. The Service has its men everywhere. No doubt a man is already here, a man who is stationed either here or somewhere in the vicinity."

"Is that why you telephoned before we started?" Ted asked.

Red Mack nodded. As the men disappeared from view, a shabby, colored man shambled up to them.

"Mistah, is you all needing anything?"

Some signal he made must have caught the

"MISTAH, IS YOU ALL NEEDING ANYTHING?"

observant Red's eye. The latter opened his coat and flashed his badge.

The old negro showed his own. "Mr. Nixon sent me," He spoke naturally now, without trace of dialect. "What do you think of my make-up?" he added.

"It's perfect," replied Mack. "My name is Mack," he added. "This young man is Ted Marsh."

"My name is Fowler," the man replied as he nodded in greeting to the boy.

Then he recounted what Nixon had ordered him to do.

"When I got word as to the coming of these men up here I suspected it was to raise trouble among the darkies. Then, when I saw the colored brethren at the station I felt certain of it. Luckily your train was reported late, so I had time to dress for the occasion.

"These darkies are to meet at the colored fraternal hall. First they are having a dinner. The colored folks are proud of the fact that white folks will eat with them. After that comes the meeting."

"How can we get into the meeting?" asked Mack.

"We can't," replied Fowler. "But we can get all the information we want from one of the negroes present!"

"That will have to do," assented Mack.

"Wouldn't a dictaphone come in handy?" Ted remarked with the memory of the one he had used in Chicago.

CHAPTER XXIII

THE NET DRAWS CLOSER

TED'S mind was active now.

"Say, Mr. Fowler," he remarked in the midst of a discussion the two men were having, as to what could be done.

"Do you know the room in which they are to hold the meeting?"

"Yes, I do," was the reply. "That was one of the first things I found out when I got here."

"Any chance for me to be stowed away somewhere in there?"

"I hardly think so," said Fowler slowly, bringing again to his mind the picture of the big room. "No," he added, "I don't know of a place in there where you could be secreted."

"Suppose we take another look?" Mack suggested. "Even if your colored friend gives us the information, we shall need verification."

"No, it won't hurt to look again," Fowler agreed, "especially since it is but a little way beyond this square."

They entered the building which was quiet and empty. The big room took the entire ground floor.

Red Mack made a careful inspection of the room but he was unsuccessful in finding any place that would prove suitable for hiding. Ted, however, was making a hunt for himself.

"Here, Red," he suddenly called, "help me move this."

Red did so. Fowler also helped. The three moved a platform which ran the height of three steps and on which were the ceremonial seats of the officers.

"This is fine," said Ted. "I can almost sit up straight here."

"It's dangerous, too dangerous," objected Mack. "If these men find you—they are desperate, you know."

"But they won't," the boy replied. "There

is just room enough there for me, although," he added, "I should like it more if it had some air holes."

"That's easily done," replied Fowler. He pulled out a sharp knife and on that side of the platform which was against the wall be managed, after considerable effort to cut a large hole.

"This should give you air," he remarked.

"Here, Ted," Mack said seriously, "take this gun. Try to fall asleep for an hour or two, for you are going to have an uncomfortable evening. If you have any trouble at all, use the gun. We shall be near by and ready at a second's notice."

"It's time to go," said Fowler, who was watching the street through the window.

"Good bye, Ted," Red Mack called in a low voice.

After the two men left, Ted made himself as comfortable as he could. He tried to fall asleep but although he dozed fitfully, he finally decided that because of the discomfort it would be useless for him to tempt sleep.

Yet, tempted or not, sleep must have

come, for he suddenly awakened with a start. He realized that the room was occupied. Men were in earnest conversation. There was the sound throughout the room of moving, scraping chairs. He tried to move but his body felt stiff. Cautiously he finally moved his left limb which had fallen asleep. It relieved the torture of his position, somewhat.

"How long have I been sleeping?" he wondered. But he found no means of telling. The men seemed to have been there for quite a time.

"I'm just a plain sleepy-head," he thought. "A nice report I would have had to make if I had slept much longer."

At first the voices were but an indistinct part of the general noise. Then Ted gradually began to make out the words. Soon he heard quite clearly.

The man who had been speaking, a darky, sat down. Then he, who no doubt was the chairman, announced:

"Our friend, Mr. Schoen, will take the floor."

Schoen went into a long harangue. He

flattered the negroes, spoke of their equality with the whites. He told them that no white man had reason to feel his superiority. The Germans, he added, gave equal rights in fact, as well as in theory, to all men.

"Everywhere, you men whose skin happens to be differently colored from mine, will rise and demand equal rights. The American has been your oppressor. Throw off his yoke, demand the things that are rightfully yours. Germany will come to your help, so will Mexico, so will Japan."

The negroes listened, flattered. Other speakers, colored and white, rose and flayed the government.

Ted's blood boiled. Here were these men enjoying the safety and protection of the United States, plotting mischief and treason.

Schoen arose once more.

"We have spoken everywhere throughout the South to the men of your race. Everywhere, our appeal has borne fruit. Success is assured. It is but a question of time."

Ted listened carefully. He knew he had sufficient evidence to convict every man there.

Then an old negro arose.

"I'se promise to keep my mouth shut when I leave here. So I will. But, my blood boils, niggers. My father was a slave before the war. This old nigger fought in a colored men's regiment against the Spaniards."

He paused for a minute, then continued:

"What made you all think I was that kind of a nigger? I allow Uncle Sam hasn't treated us niggers any too well, but things are tolerably improved, and better times are coming.

"These Germans come here. They think niggers have no sense so they do their best to have niggers make trouble. Only no account folks, will make trouble for Uncle Sam, now."

The Germans made no comment, but Ted heard much shuffling of feet after the darky had completed his remarks.

"I reckon Uncle Mose is right," said one.

But only a few ventured to make any such comment. They were pledged to secrecy by such an oath that it would have taken all of Uncle Sam's forces to bring out a confession. Negroes are terrified into secrecy by the awful fear of hoodooism.

Outside, Red Mack and Fowler kept watch for more than an hour. At the end of that time, it was decided by the two men that Fowler should get the Chief of Police and make arrests. There seemed no doubt in the minds of either of the men that the evidence would be forthcoming.

It was after eleven o'clock when the men started to leave the room. The Germans had already effected a temporary organization among the negroes and a meeting had been announced for the following Wednesday.

CHAPTER XXIV

The Capture

WHEN the last man had departed, Ted found himself so stiff and cramped that it was impossible to move. It took several minutes to restore the circulation of his blood. Muscle sore, he moved the platform with a great effort and managed to force his way from under it.

Outside of the house an exciting episode was taking place.

As the men made their way out of the building they found themselves confronted by a number of policemen and a few men in civilian clothes.

"You are all under arrest," the chief announced.

A second's silence followed. The negroes

became panic-stricken. Not so the four Germans. Without an attempt at explanation, they made a mad dash into the building again.

"Quick," said Mack. "The other side of the house."

Fowler and three officers raced around the building.

Mack had guessed the plan of the men. It was to get into the big room again. From there the chance of escape was not impossible.

Ted, lame and stiff, was coming out of the room. He saw these men rushing toward the door. Quick as a flash he slammed it shut. As the men crashed into it, the bolt caught. The door held.

The Germans at bay, turned. Red Mack was upon them. The policemen were close on his heels.

One of the trapped men attempted to fire but Mack knocked the gun out of his hands. He closed in on this man, even as the officers, clubs drawn, bore down upon the three others.

Mack's man was no match for him. Red landed a short uppercut on his chin and the man dropped.

But the policemen were somewhat clumsy, even though the Teutons were outnumbered.

Red turned to give them help, but although the officers were sorely put to it, they were getting their prisoners well in hand.

Mack then knocked on the closed door and called out.

"Oh, Ted, don't you allow your friends to call?"

Ted opened the door, a wide grin on his face.

"Don't think I wasn't watching. I saw some of it through the keyhole. That is, I was at the keyhole until I heard some men trying to climb the wall. Can't make out who they are."

"Those are our men," Mack replied. "We were sure that the Germans would make their break through this room and out of those windows when they bolted. They would have, too, if you had not slammed the door in their faces."

"They certainly seemed to be coming fast. For one second I thought the bolt wouldn't catch in time," he boy answered.

"Did you gather any information?" Red asked him as Fowler joined them.

Ted told them briefly of what the Germans had tried to do and something of the plans as he had heard them.

As the boy was describing the meeting, he suddenly thought of the negro who had protested against it all.

"Where are the prisoners?" he asked Red.

"Over there," was the reply. "Want to see them?"

The negroes were loud in their bewailings and protestations of innocence. Only one darky kept quiet, making no comment. Only once, was he heard to speak.

"Serves you darkies right," he remarked tersely.

"Uncle," said Ted, as he walked over to him, "are you the darky who didn't belong to that crowd?"

"White boy, how do you know? Didn't seem to do no good nohow to tell these white folks about not belonging there, so I didn't.

"Young master, just tell them I ain't that kind of a nigger, will you?" he continued.

Ted did. He explained to Fowler, Red and

the chief and told them of the speech the darky had made.

"Well," said Red Mack, "you certainly do not belong with this crowd, Uncle. You are a respectable colored man. So go your way."

The other negroes watched the old man departing.

Then they set up a further loud bewailing. But it did them no good. The patrol made three trips and the white men were included in the very first of these.

A few days later Ted and Red offered their evidence. So did one of the negroes who had been present at the meeting as well as the old darky who had been freed through the testimony of Ted.

Not very long after that, the Germans were sent to prison for treason. The case against them was complete and they had nothing at all to say when permission was given them to make a statement.

CHAPTER XXV

TED'S FRIENDS CALL

THERE followed days of great activity for Ted and his two friends, Jerome and Benton. Red Mack had been sent to New Orleans for a number of days. He had received special mention for his work in capturing the Germans and he stood in line for promotion.

But he had no desire for the same. Such service as he could give, he gave gladly. But his plans were to return to the mine at the earliest moment.

For this man, only twenty-six, had decided that he was no longer to follow the fickle dictates of fancy but to stick to the one road that leads to success. Nor was success measured by him in the same sense as it is measured by many of us. For him, success meant the fulfillment of ideals, of plans, modest in themselves, yet worthy of desire and accomplishment. So that, although promotion promised, he knew that with all its call, he would not stay in the Service. Such time was coming when he would join one of Uncle Sam's fighting forces.

That time would be soon. He had talked it over with Ted, Ted who was even then so closely associated with the army.

"Do you know, Ted, I know nothing of the navy, but when I volunteer, I shall go into the marines. For, if I am to fight for Uncle Sam, I want that fighting to come soon."

Red Mack had also voiced Ted's desire. The army held a strong fascination for the boy. Those strong, cool, capable men who were in it made him feel that it was indeed a worthwhile profession. 'And yet, in his mind, there was the vague hope that when duty called—he would be allowed a place as one of Uncle Sam's Navy Boys. With all that, his love for the army was strong.

Jerome and Benton were in high hopes that they too would be allowed in the Officers' Training Camp as mascots. But Captain Perkins decided that he could make no further exceptions and so the two boys found themselves outside the pale.

But Ted, at such times when they were allowed to visit him, gave them a thorough account of what work he had to do and the things that were happening.

"See those men," Ted pointed out a group one Saturday afternoon.

"They don't look happy, do they?" remarked Jerome.

"No, they don't. They've been rejected. Some little thing is the matter with each of them."

The camp meant training for three months and the plans were to make officers of those men who were finally enrolled.

"Captain Perkins is strict. He does not excuse the least break. But, it's good for us," Ted had added. "You see, we're supposed to make officers—and that is the way he teaches us to make good ones."

"Just think, Jerome," Benton remarked wonderingly, "how much it takes to make an officer."

Then squad drill came on. The two boys were allowed to watch, and although the men practiced mostly with broom sticks, the boys felt a thrill of pride. They began to understand the meaning of patriotism, what love of country meant.

"Don't think for a minute," Ted told them after the drill was over, "that it's easy. It isn't. Want to know what we do?"

"Tell us," said Benton.

"Well," was the reply, "reveille's at 6:15. 'Assembly is fifteen minutes later. Not much chance for cleaning up, is there? After you have answered to your name, there is 'setting up' exercise. That's great fun," Ted added. "And it makes you hungry.

"Breakfast is a little after 7:00. Then beds have to be made and they have to be perfect. You can't get away with anything. Captain Perkins is too wise.

"Drill is at eight. From nine to ten we're free. Captain Perkins talks to us then and its always a good straight talk. We all learn lots.

"Dinner at a quarter after noon. Drill for more than an hour and a half—from two to half past three. Retreat at 5:30, then we have review or parade for about half an hour. Supper is at a quarter past six. I usually study after supper. Some of the men just loaf.

"At quarter to ten taps—they give you fifteen minutes until they sound taps."

"It's hard, I guess," Jerome remarked, "but Ted, I wish I could be in it."

"So do I," said his brother.

"Well, Jerome, I'll play you some tennis," said Ted, changing the subject.

"Attaboy," was the eager acceptance of the challenge.

They began a spirited game. Tennis was the thing that Ted's opponent could play best. Ted, who had learned the game, could not play nearly as well as the younger boy. Several of the men came over and watched. Ted played hard. He did not give up easily. It was not in his nature to do so.

"Our Ted is a sticker," remarked one of the bystanders to another.

"He's not easily beaten for one thing. Any other lad would have been beaten at once, but not Ted."

"I'll bet the other boy will know he's been in a game."

The games were now three to two with forty love. The next serve Ted answered and made a difficult return. Jerome missed and the score stood 40—15. Ted won the next, then the next which made it deuce. He went to love but lost the next on service. Jerome won the next two after that. He played brilliantly.

So each of the next four games was contested. Ted lost the game, the score being 6 to 4.

"Good boy, Ted," called the victor.

"You're a crackerjack player," was the answer. Let's play another."

The second game, equally close, Ted won.

"Good boy, Ted," the men called loyally. They were extremely proud of him and liked his way in defeat and in victory.

CHAPTER XXVI

A PICNIC

WORD came a day or so later that General Pershing had been assigned to the command of the army in France. Ted was greatly interested. He felt a great pride in the rugged general; he was proud that he was one who knew him well.

"It will be great to be in the trenches with him in command."

Of course, it was but a dream. Ted was entirely too young and it was hardly possible that the good fortune which had attended him up to now and which had gotten him into the training camp, despite his extreme youth, would continue to follow. Yet, no one could blame him for wishing and dreaming for things as he would want them.

Ted was learning with a quickness that

THE CANOE MADE ITS WAY DOWN STREAM

came naturally to him, and no one in the camp was more proficient than this boy.

"Our young soldier will make a great mascot," remarked Tom Hardy who was in line for a lieutenancy. He had grown fond of Ted, as had all the men, and he had taken him under his wing.

Whenever the opportunity offered, the Day boys came over for Ted. A picnic had been planned for a certain Saturday morning. Since it was Ted's free time he went off with them. The three boys had been planning this picnic for many a day.

The father of the Day boys reluctantly agreed to let them use his canoe, one that had been given to him by an Indian and which he prized highly.

The canoe made its way down stream. Benton and Jerome paddling, Ted in the stern, they made fair progress.

They were bound for a point which had been suggested by one of the men who was in Mr. Day's employ, a man who had become quite friendly to both Jerome and Benton. He was a new man but he did his work to the satisfaction of everyone and so although Mr. Day had formed a prejudice against Robbins, he was ready to admit he had no good foundation for the prejudice.

"Yet I can't stand for any American's making it a point to associate with Mexicans. Robbins does so."

The boat came close to shore. Their destination was still many miles away but the boys enjoyed every bit of the trip. Without any desire that its termination be hastened, they came close to shore and drifted alongside the bank.

"How about a swim?" Benton suggested.

"Goody," said Jerome. "Let's do it."

Ted looked about. It was a quiet spot, so he agreed. The three paddled into shore, lifted the canoe onto some branches and in two seconds were disrobed.

They had a wonderful swim, after which they paddled on. Noon, when the sun blazed directly overhead, found them at their destination.

"I'm hungry, aren't you?" said Ted.

"You bet," they both replied.

"All right, then, let's get our meal. Suppose we had nothing and had to find our food? Shall we hunt for it?"

The other two boys agreed, but with a longing look at the food in hand.

"Benton, you and I will see what game we can find. Jerome, you go out and see what kind of a fisherman you are. Whichever one falls down on getting some food will have to serve the other two."

The three boys were off on the duties assigned.

Luck was with the two, for they had not cut into the woods for more than a mile when Ted pointed out some wild fowl to the younger boy.

"Shoot," he called. Benton did, but he missed. Ted had shot a second later and was more successful.

"Well, that's some dinner," remarked Benton. "Wonder if I'm going to do the serving?" he added.

Another opportunity, however, was given

them within the ten minutes. This time Ted did not fire at all and Benton winged one of the birds. He killed it with a second shot.

"All right, let's get back before Jerome," Benton called excitedly. But alas, that young man was already there, cleaning two fish.

"Well, I'll serve," said Benton. "It's up to me."

"I'm cook and Jerome will bring the water, so I guess we'll have enough to do," said Ted.

But it was more than an hour before the meal was ready.

"It's the best eats I've ever had," said Benton.

"Better than the eats you had at Aunt Cala's. Remember?" Jerome asked.

"When was that?" asked Ted interested.

"Benton came home one day," said his brother. "He told mother that Aunt Cala knew how to take care of boys. His feet were soaked, so she took off his shoes and stockings, dried them, made him comfortable in a big chair. I guess she fussed over him a lot. When she was all done, what do you think Benton said?"

"What?" asked Ted.

" 'All right, Aunt Cala. Bring on the eats.' "

Ted laughed long and loud.

"Mother was horrified, as you can guess," Jerome concluded.

CHAPTER XXVII

BENTON IS KIDNAPPED

THE boys had decided to return home at sundown. They found great fun in loafing and talking of things that had happened and each one told of his plans.

"I like it down here," Ted said. "But I haven't found any place that's as good as the Double X."

"That's in Canada, isn't it?" Benton inquired.

Ted nodded. "It's great up there. You know, it's cold in the winter time. When I first came out there, Smiles was foreman. Mr. Dean thought a lot of him. Then the war came and many of the men who were citizens of Canada went off to France.

"Smiles was killed. I'll bet he died with a

smile. He was a great man. He met everything in a happy spirit. He was good to me, too, when I was green and knew nothing of what had to be done at a ranch. Want me to tell you what Red Mack did because he knew he could count on Smiles?"

"Go ahead," the two boys replied eagerly.

"Well," said Ted, "there was McGowan who had a gang of cattle thieves. A reckless lot; they would go on a rampage and when pursued would race to the other side of the border, the Canadian line, you know. And, if the pursuit was on the other side, they would change about.

"They had made considerable trouble and so clever and reckless were they, it was almost impossible to get them. McGowan was the only one of the entire gang who was known.

"One night, Red Mack decided to investigate. He had an idea he knew where the gang was located, but Mack hates to say anything unless he's sure. He didn't want the cowboys to follow him to the place he suspected and then find it was a fool's errand. Not he.

"Instead, he asked me if I'd take a ride. Didn't tell me where or on what errand we were bound, just asked if I would ride. Did I accept? Well, I guess I did.

"When we arrived near the point Red was bound for, he told me about the McGowan gang and what he suspected. Then he did as cool a thing as I've ever heard about. He wanted to make sure it was McGowan and not peaceable strangers, so he told me, he'd walk in on them as if he had no thought that they were anything but friendly. I was to listen. If I gathered it was McGowan from the talk that followed, I was to crawl back to my horse, Scout. His own horse, Brownie, he had allowed to graze at some point.

" 'Go for Smiles,' he told me. 'He and the men can't hurry any too fast to suit me, for things will be interesting while I'm visiting McGowan.'

"He planned that Smiles was to send Brownie, Mack's horse, forward to the gang's cave as soon as he was ready to attack. After that, they were to be on the watch until Red gave the signal.

"I guess you can imagine how fast I rode. In the meantime, Red just jollied McGowan and his men. They couldn't make out just what he was there for but finally decided that he had strayed in.

"Smiles and the men rode at breakneck speed until they were within two miles of the cave. They then moved forward as silently as Indians.

"They found Brownie and sent him forward to the cave. The outlaws jumped at first, then decided it was just that the horse had been grazing and had come to his master.

"While we were watching we could hear Red talking naturally and quietly and all the outlaws ill at ease and awfully suspicious. They didn't know what to do.

"Then suddenly there was a crash, the cave was pitch dark. We didn't dare shoot, of course, because Red Mack was there. But the outlaws did. A few seconds later we heard Mack's welcome voice.

" 'I reckon, Smiles, you can go to it', he called. He had escaped. He had kicked the lamp over so that it would be pitch dark, and in the confusion had managed to make his exit.

"Smiles gathered in the whole McGowan gang. They made a fight at first but soon realized they were trapped and gave in."

"You say Smiles was killed?" Jerome asked.

"Yes, the Canadians made a wonderful charge in one of the battles on the Somme and Smiles was one of a large number killed. Mr. Dean had been wounded and had been sent home."

"We'll be fighting soon, too," won't we?" Benton asked soberly.

"We certainly will. But, it's great when you can fight for a country like ours, isn't it?" Ted replied.

The boys then took a twenty minute walk. Returning, they were surprised to see an automobile nearby. Around their fire, which was now but live coals, were a number of men.

"Hello, Robbins," Jerome called, for he had recognized the man in their employ. "What are you doing here?"

"Your father wants you two boys to go

with us," was the man's reply. "He sent us for you. Your mother is sick at home."

Benton and Jerome looked at each other uncertain.

"Better go home in the boat," Ted remarked suspiciously. "It will take but a little longer."

"He told me to bring you," Robbins replied disagreeably. "Here you," and he turned to Ted with a snarl, "you go in the boat if you wish—we'll go in the car. At any rate, keep out of this."

"Well, these boys won't go with you." Ted looked squarely in the man's eye. "Will you?" he turned to the boys.

"No, we won't. We'll go home with Ted. You can tell father that."

"You won't?" the man replied with an oath. "Get them, boys."

The attack was so sudden, that the men had hold of the boys in a few seconds' time. After the first shock, however, the three boys began again to struggle.

Ted managed to free himself from his man.

As the man bore down on him, he dodged quickly, the man falling over him. Immediately Ted turned to Jerome's captor.

In but a flash he was on him. Jerome was doing his best. The two managed to keep the man occupied. Jerome felt himself free and burst from the man's grasp. So did Ted. Benton, the smallest, however, was being held safely by two men. He did a brave thing on the spur of the moment.

"Run," he called. "Get help."

"Quick," Ted called to Jerome, "this way."

They rushed to the canoe and pushed off.

"Wonder what they'll do to Benton?" Jerome asked, tears in his voice.

"Nothing," Ted answer. "Where's the nearest house that has a telephone?"

"Over there, about two miles," Jerome replied. "They're the Stoddards."

Ted paddled swiftly.

"I think they intend to kidnap Benton and hold him for a ransom. It's up to us to get in touch with a telephone and get everybody everywhere to watch."

They beached the canoe and hurried to the house. Mr. Stoddard came to the door.

"Hello, Jerome, what's the trouble?"

"Benton has been kidnapped and we want to use the telephone."

Ted called for long distance. While the call was being rushed through, Ted briefly explained what had happened.

"Know the number of the car?" asked the man.

"Yes, sir," Ted replied. "It's T87613."

"That's right," Jerome said. "That's the number."

"Good—they'll have a task to make their escape."

Mr. Day took the news quietly. "I shall telephone to all points, east, west and north. Put Mr. Stoddard on."

After the latter had completed his conversation he called his men together.

"Watch the river, boys. Make it a half mile watch. That will mean you can cover 5 miles."

Ted asked permission to telephone Captain Perkins.

"May I stay with the hunting party?" he asked.

"No, Ted, you and Jerome come here. It will give the men in the camp some work and we'll also make our try to capture the kidnappers. You two may be able to help us."

When Ted told Mr. Stoddard what Captain Perkins had instructed him to do, the latter approved the plan at once. He brought out his car and within the hour the boys had reported to the captain.

CHAPTER XXVIII

The Rescue

ROBBINS was in bad humor as was clearly apparent.

"A nice lot you are. Milk sops. To let two boys make their escape. Couldn't handle two boys, huh?" he growled in disgust.

"Well, mine was a tartar," the one who had handled Ted replied. "He was too quick for me. I noticed he managed to get the boy away from the Mexican, too," he added, finding some satisfaction in the failure of one of the other men.

"Those boys were quick. They move just like that," and the Mexican snapped his finger to give evidence of their speed.

"Well, no post-mortems. Here Pete," Robbins called to the Mexican. "Give me the other automobile number to put on."

"Why?" asked the other man. "You don't suppose those boys found time to read our number, do you?"

"I don't know whether they did or didn't, but I'm not going to be caught napping. It may be that those boys were fools. It may be, that they just paddle home. However, they may also have telephoned to Day. He would then telephone and telegraph everywhere.

"So, here's what's to be done. Now that the number is changed, I want you to hide the boy at the cabin. Then we, that is Pete and myself, will go on with the car and try to make connections over in Mexico, so that we can take the boy over there. All we have to do then is to wait until Day comes across. It would have been much quicker and easier though, if you hadn't let those boys get away."

In the next half hour the automobile was making its way north. It was stopped once or twice but the number not being the one they had first, and with no evidence about of a boy, they were allowed to pass.

"I guess they know the number all right," Robbins chuckled, after one of these stops. "Nothing like taking every precaution."

He managed to make his way into El Paso. But from El Paso he sent two other men across the bridge to negotiate for concealing the boy. There was the probability, he decided, that some member of the Day household or even one of the boys would be on watch.

As a matter of fact, Captain Perkins had stationed Ted and Tom Hardy at this point. The two were watching each car as it turned to the bridge.

"There comes a Mitchell that looks very much like our car," Ted suddenly announced, pointing to a car. "But the men aren't the same," he added, disappointed.

"Then it probably isn't the car," Hardy replied.

Ted, nevertheless, took a closer look, but found no sign to indicate that it was anything but a strange car.

The man and the boy kept their station until late that evening. The same car returned, and was stopped by the customs officials.

"I'm going to follow them," said Ted, still suspicious.

"It may be nothing, but then no other clue has come up, so far."

Hardy agreed. The boy stole up and seated himself on the back of the car where the two men on the inside could not see him.

The car started off. After a mile or so out of town, the car turned into a lane. Ted dropped off. The man who was driving, tooted his horn twice and got out. Another man came to the door of the house.

"What luck?" he asked. "Will they keep him?"

"Yes, they will," the other responded.

Ted joyfully realized that the clue had proved worth while. "Him" he decided must mean Benton.

"But they want $3,000," the first speaker continued.

"They don't want much, do they? Well, it's so much more for old Day to pay."

"If you're ready," Robbins continued, "we'll go to the cabin."

It was a muscle-sore Ted who dropped off

when the car slowed up, at the kidnappers' hiding place. He hid again although the darkness in itself made a welcome protection.

The two men sat down on the veranda. Ted waited for over a half hour, then he approached with the utmost caution. So close did he crawl that he could hear the words of the speaker.

"It's good for at least $15,000, Carroll," Robbins was saying. "But it will be lost if we make a hasty or ill-timed move. It's so much harder because we allowed those boys to get away."

"Well, we can wait for ten days," Carroll replied.

"Yes, and longer, if necessary. We'll take the boy over the border tomorrow. We'll have to keep him under cover, though."

"Who's watching him?" Robbins asked one of the other men.

"He's safe enough. He's up on that top floor room. It would be an impossible drop, even if the window wasn't too high for him to reach."

"Well, I'd keep my eye on him, at that,"

Robbins replied. "There's many a slip 'twixt the cup and the lip."

Ted found that the so-called cabin was a two-story farmhouse. Now he crawled to the back of the building and cautiously prowled about. He came to the barn and entered. It was too dark to see but he felt about. He found some straw in one corner. Near a stall his hands came upon a coil of rope.

Exultantly, the boy made sure it was of sufficient length and strength.

"I wonder how I can manage to get up there," Ted thought to himself as he glanced to the top of the building in which the men and Benton were housed. "Wonder, too, which room it is?"

But, upon a further careful and thorough inspection he noticed that one of the windows on the upper floor was about three feet higher than the others.

"That must be the room," Ted decided. He remembered that one of the men had spoken of the high window.

Never before had Ted had such a long and nervous wait. He did not dare attempt any rescue until the men had gone to sleep. This they did not do for an hour.

Then it was necessary to make sure that enough time had been given them in which to fall asleep. It was after three o'clock, with just a trace of the dawn coming from the eastern sky, when Ted, who had managed to unweave enough strands from the rope to make a fair-sized cord with which to raise it, climbed to the first floor. That was easy. He raised the rope to the top of the veranda. Benton's room, however, was on the other side of the building. There was no way in which to get to it, from where Ted was. Ted sat down, disappointed.

"Why, I'll climb to the roof," he suddenly thought. "From there, it may be easy."

Ted now removed his shoes, so that he would not make any noise. Then he shinned up the rain pipe. This was not hard. Once on the roof, he crawled over to the side of the building in which was the window he was after.

He looked down and could see that one shutter was swinging in the breeze.

CAREFULLY HE LET HIMSELF DOWN

Suppose," he thought, "there's a man in the room with Benton? Suppose it isn't Benton's room?"

The dawn began to show a little stronger.

"I'll have to chance it," Ted decided.

He lifted up the rope with the thin strands he had tied together. Thanks to the teachings at the ranch, he managed to make an effective lasso about the big chimney. He brought the rope to the edge immediately above the window. Then carefully he let himself down. When he came to the window he perched himself on the sill.

The dim light played into the room. Ted saw a man fast asleep, snoring heavily.

In the furthermost corner, Ted also saw with great relief, the figure of his small friend. He let himself quietly, stealthily into the room. As noiselessly as a mouse he made his way toward the man. He stepped over him. The man moved. Ted flattened himself against the wall. By the man's side the boy saw a gun. He bent down and picked it up. The man slept on.

Then Ted moved over to the boy's side.

One hand touched the other ready to smother any outcry.

Benton opened his eyes. He evidently did not remember where he was for the moment. When it dawned on him, he was already accustomed to the figure standing above him.

Ted, finger on lip, cautioned silence and pointed to the window.

Benton, a world of questions in his eyes, still a little dazed, nodded that he understood.

Ted and he crawled to the window. Ted saw the younger boy slide down safely, then he himself came down.

"This way, Benton," he whispered.

And then Ted did the most brazen, daring act of all. He led the way to the automobile.

A grin spread over Benton's face as he realized Ted's intention.

"Oh, boy, you're a wonder. But can't we honk the horn and then fly?" he begged.

Ted realized that they could not start the car without awakening one or two of the men. Very thoroughly he made sure of the car's readiness to start. When his preparations were completed, he honked his horn, loud and long.

The next minute they were off, past the house. They had the satisfaction of seeing Robbins and two of the men rush to the door. Benton waved his hat. Ted gave the car more gas and it rapidly picked up speed.

Robbins made a fruitless dash, realized the uselessness of it and shook his fist at the fast disappearing machine.

CHAPTER XXIX

Ted and Benton Return

TED explained to his friend how he had found him and something of the search that had been made. It was almost seven when Ted, who had had a blowout on the way, drove through the Day gateway. The boys had not stopped to telephone.

Mrs. Day had spent a sleepless night.

The father, looking worried and distressed, came to the door.

Ted and Benton stood there.

"What?" Mr. Day gasped. "What?"

"Yes, it's Benton," said that worthy. "I thought it was time to come home."

The father took him in his arms and gave him a great bear's hug. The mother had already appeared and she took her youngest son in her arms and in pure happiness and content, wept over him.

"How did it happen?" asked the father.

"I'll bet Ted had something to do with it," said Jerome, who also had appeared.

"You win," said Benton. "He had everything to do with it."

"Now, tell us your part," said Mr. Day to Ted. He spoke very quietly, but there was a great feeling of gratitude within him.

Ted gave a modest account of what he had done, how he had picked out and followed the car.

"I was certainly lucky," he said. "They call me Lucky as you know, and my nick-name has proved it's truth again."

When he came to the part where the two had slid down the rope, Benton interrupted him and continued the story.

"The best part was where we tooted the horn to tell them we were going."

"That was clever work, Ted," Mr. Day told him. "It was a splendid idea to take away from them and use for yourself the only thing they had with which to pursue you."

"May I call up Captain Perkins?" the boy asked.

"Yes, and I want to talk to him, too," the father of Benton added.

Ted called up his captain.

"This is Ted," the boy announced.

"My," was the answer. "Hardy is worried over you. He told me that you had followed a car, that he had said it would be all right, unthinkingly. He doesn't know what's happened to you."

"Well, captain, that was the car, and Benton is safely home now."

"He's home. How did he get home?" asked the astounded officer.

Ted told him how in a few words.

"You young rascal," the captain commented. "I'm proud of you."

"Captain, Mr. Day wants to talk to you. Just a minute."

Mr. Day got on the line. He asked the captain when he could see him and then he hung up the receiver.

"I suppose you're going back to camp now, Ted. I shall see you later in the day."

Mr. Day walked down the road with the boy. The two boys wanted to go too, but he told them that they could see Ted later.

"Ted, I'm extremely grateful to you. I owe you a lot. I want you to know you can count on me through thick and thin, at any time. I am not going to offer you any reward for this—because it is beyond anything that is paid for in that way. But count on me at all times."

"I'm glad, sir," replied the boy, "to have your friendship."

"Well, I'll see you later, my boy. We must take steps at once to corral the villains. Tell Captain Perkins that I have reported it to the police office and am myself going out with a number of men. I shall appreciate any assistance from him."

The captain was waiting for the boy. He shook hands warmly. Then he sent for Hardy.

"Where have you been?" he asked. "I was worried to a frazzle."

Captain Perkins told him. Tom Hardy listened.

"And to think I let this boy go off and do all this by himself. If ever a *next time comes!*" he added ruefully.

Ted gave Mr. Day's message to the captain. The latter listened, then commented:

"I'll see what I can do, Ted. But we can't interfere too much in these things. We're not supposed to."

A widespread net was placed for the kidnappers. The local authorities telegraphed to all the towns within a radius of two hundred miles.

About noon, two days later, word came that three men had been arrested who fitted the description. Ted and Mr. Day boarded a train at once. It proved to be Robbins, Pete and one of the other men.

When Mr. Day and Ted walked in on Robbins, the latter greeted them cheerfully.

"Oh, I deserve it," he said. "To let a boy

like him get the best of me.   To have him add insult to injury and take my car to escape, too.

"No, I hold no grudge.   We fellows who try these stunts must take our punishment.   But, after seemingly looking out for everything, to be beaten by a kid."

When Mr. Day returned, the car was still at the house.   In talking it over with the chief of police, the latter said he did not intend to make any claim for it until a demand was made on him.   So Mr. Day told Ted to make use of it until further notice.

Ted did, you may be sure.

CHAPTER XXX

The Corps Pays a Visit

MR. DAY called on Captain Perkins to discuss the future of Ted. The former was anxious to have Ted stay with him for a year or more. But Captain Perkins felt that Ted was better off where he was. He had a great belief in the value of military training and there were few boys, so he told Mr. Day, who could get the training that Ted was getting. So Mr. Day agreed.

Now, conscription day was but a day away. There were a number of Indians in New Mexico who had threatened trouble. They would not register, so they said, and several of them had already made an attempt to escape into Mexico.

It was the declared intention of the government to have everyone between 21 and 30 register and the United States officials had kept a sharp eye on slackers. Orders had been sent to Captain Perkins to be prepared to hurry into Andredo where the Indian camp was located. At sundown, Monday, June 4th, a message came to the captain and he immediately sent out a call. In the space of five minutes, the men were ready.

They boarded the train. The trip to Aldredo was long but uneventful. The men arrived after midnight and made camp at once.

Early morning brought the inspiring call of the reveille. The men answered at once. Then flags flying, drums and fifes playing Yankee Doodle, they paraded down to the Indian camp. Three hundred strong, they presented a picture which made the truculent Indians think again before refusing to register.

By no word or action did Captain Perkins or any of the men give any hint of the purpose of their call. On the face of it, it was just drill. The men played about, after their regular drills, the Indians watchful but silent.

Only one Indian, a grizzled and worn old brave, was heard to make a comment.

"Plenty of young bucks, heap fools." He

meant the Indians who had threatened not to register.

Close of day found every Indian, whose age was within the required limits, accounted for.

When the day was ended, the captain with seven men, one of whom was our friend Ted, paid his respects to the chief.

The Indian conversed in words of one syllable.

He was specially interested in Ted.

"He heap young buck," he said.

Captain Perkins agreed.

"Make very good brave," was his answer. "Very good."

The Indian continued to watch Ted who was also interested in these Indians, who were so unlike those that inhabited Alberta and the rest of Western Canada.

The chief, who had volunteered no comment on the visit of the soldiers, made but one remark, touching it as his visitors left.

"The white man, if he seeks the source of the river, should look for it where the hills are high and not in the middle or the end."

"I wonder what the fox meant," said Captain Perkins as they reached their camp.

"I never was good at puzzles," said Hardy. None of the other men could sense the meaning.

"I think I know, captain," said Ted. "It is this: as to the reason for our coming, we should look elsewhere for the root of the trouble. I suppose he means among the Germans or Mexicans."

"That is it, I am sure," replied the captain.

"You see, captain, all Indians talk that way and up North we used to see a lot of them, so we sort of grew accustomed to their talk."

The men stayed until the following morning. To Ted it was a night, the memory of which would stay long with him. The camp fire blazed, the men sat about, the shadows playing fitfully on their suits of khaki.

As is usual in such cases, the men told their experiences.

Captain Perkins strolled toward the group while the talk was going on. He sat down a little outside the circle. He puffed at his pipe and also listened.

"We're telling experiences, captain," said Hardy. "We'd like to hear some of yours if you feel like telling them.

The captain made no answer for a few minutes.

"It's a night like this that makes you think with a thankful thrill of all the things life holds for you. A wonderful night, truly. God's country and may He keep it free from devastation.

"That's a selfish wish, but it is this country rather than our cousins across the water, who have always gladly and cheerfully given. Witness Cuba, witness our buying the Islands from Denmark, witness the money we have paid Panama.

"But I'm coming back to the last war, that little scrimmage with Spain. And, mind you, I am not talking of my own experiences. I speak of, well, let's call him Jimmy Allison.

"Jimmy was senior, the year I entered, the year just before the war. Let's see, that must have been '97.

"A wild lad was Jimmy, but the old men were glad to pal with him and we youngsters looked up to him. He was, we thought, the ideal fellow. He had every earmark of a coming great man.

"Hazing, at that time, was thought to be a necessary part of the curriculum. The officials winked at it. We new men expected it. We took it as a matter of course. It isn't so long ago, after all, about twenty years. We looked forward to the time when we in turn would do the hazing.

"To come back to Jimmy. Though reckless and wasteful of his time, he passed high in his studies. He was quick; it all came easily and naturally to him, so it seemed to us. He came from a family whose men had been represented in the college generation after generation.

"Jimmy became the leader of all the deviltry at Clayton, and yet the students loved him, despite his escapades and the trouble he made.

"It was a short time after our entrance into the war. Rooming with me was Dwight Larkins, a fellow about my own age. He came from the same town as Allison— and, this I didn't know at the time—it was

Ruth Larkins to whom Jimmy had given his loyal and devoted heart. She didn't know it; she never knew it. But now, I'm running ahead of my story.

"My turn to be hazed came and I took it. I was sick for two weeks for they had me walk for three miles bare-footed, after dark. It was winter, so you can imagine. My feet were almost frozen. What saved them was the fact that I ran all the way. I cut them to ribbons but at least they weren't frozen.

"Dwight had been furious when they brought me home. He told the men then and there that he would never be hazed. He would fight any of them but not one of them could haze him.

"Jimmy had come forward when Dwight had defied the crowd of hazers. Mischief was in his eye. 'You shall be hazed on Tuesday after next. Youngsters should be seen, not heard. We are your betters. Tuesday after next, remember.'

"The Tuesday came. Dwight had vowed he would kill the man who laid hands on him. That night Allison and ten other men came on the boy. He was ready for them.

"Well, to make the story of the tragedy brief, Dwight Larkins died that night. He had fought them off. They had closed in on him. He had pulled out his gun and Jimmy had sprung at him to take the gun away. In the scuffle the gun went off, and so did the life of Dwight Larkins.

"Allison, I don't think comprehended it at first. He stared at the boy, just stared. Then he got up, his eyes wide and unseeing. He went to his room while several of the men brought the dead body to one of the buildings.

"Somehow, no one had the heart at first to seek Jimmy and when someone did, he had disappeared.

"I enlisted in the war. It was in Cuba I had occasion to notice a man; there was something very strange about him. The devil seemed to be haunting him. And he fought like fury in every scrimmage.

"He saw me one day, and sneaked away, but I guess the need for speaking to some one who knew it all was strong in him, so he came over. And despite the great change in him, I recognized Jimmy Allison. God, what a change!

" 'I want to die, I want to die, Perkins,' he said, 'and I can't. I seem to see Dwight everywhere. And one day I really did see his sister.'

"I lost sight of him for many years. But, three days ago I heard that the Germans had gotten him. He had died, at last. He sent word to me; he picked me, I suppose, because of my close association to Dwight.

"I said he died. And yet, men, I'll swear that one of the men we turned down the other day was Jimmy Allison. I wonder, I wonder."

CHAPTER XXXI

BACK TO THE MINE

THERE was a silence of many minutes after Captain Perkins had finished.

"Well," said one of the men, "he couldn't have been both."

"No, he couldn't. Yet, I wonder if he didn't send that report over from France so that Jimmy Allison should be accounted for as dead. Not being able to die, he wanted, at least, to have people to think of him as dead. He had that pride of family which urged him to make a new start when we entered the war. His family had been represented in every war this country has been in. For his own satisfaction, he wanted to get into this war. Perhaps no one would ever find out that an Allison had done his bit, but you see he was trying to satisfy himself, not anyone else. That's my idea of it. I may be all wrong. He may have really died in France and I may have been mistaken."

"And, of course," added Hardy, "you didn't recognize the poor devil, since he did not want to be known?"

The captain nodded.

"Why was he rejected?" asked one of the other men.

"Too old. You see, he was over forty. But I certainly hope he gets his chance."

"The poor kid that died," said another of the men.

"Poor nothing," hotly replied Hardy. "Death is a thing that comes and goes. He was out of it at least. Just think of what Allison had had to go through. Think of what he had to give up! Poor devil. He didn't whine. Some men would have found a million reasons that would let them out. Not he!"

Now there came the clear notes of the bugle. Taps. The men slowly arose and walked to their tents. There was an absence of the usual boisterousness. The story had left its deep impression.

"Well, Ted," the captain addressed the boy after bidding him good night, "if you should happen to go to West Point or Annapolis, be sure not to think it is a sign of weakness because you find that they have barred hazing."

"I won't," the boy replied soberly.

Early morning found the men on board train and returning to camp. Ted was excused upon their arrival at El Paso. When he went for his mail he found only one card. It was from Red Mack who announced that he was returning some time that day. Ted looked up the time tables and found that there were two trains due that afternoon.

Ted met the first train in the car which he had taken from the kidnappers. Red Mack was on it. His friend looked at the car, then at Ted. It was typical of Red Mack that he asked no questions.

Ted drove to a hotel where Mack engaged a room.

As Red made a chance of clothes, he said:

"Well, Ted, I'm through with the Service. We caught the men we were after. I've already sent my resignation to Washington.

"I've registered, of course," he added. "I don't know when I'll be called—hope it will be with the first draft."

"What are your plans for the present?" the boy inquired.

"I'm going to try to get Arthur and go up to our mine. It's fairly safe to start our work again. We can get through with at least two months of work before we are called."

"When are you going?" Ted asked.

"I'm going to wire Arthur today and start within the week."

"You talk as if I'm out of it," the boy said, crossly.

"Why, I figure you are. Aren't you? You belong here, Ted. It's your place."

"My place, temporarily, as yours was. I'm sure that Captain Perkins will agree with me. I also think that he will try to keep a place for me, should I come back."

"Well, Ted, it's for you to decide. I shall be glad to have you with us. I don't have to tell you that, I suppose?"

"How about father?" Ted inquired.

"We'd better let him stay at home. You see, it is at best only a temporary affair. We may be called away at any minute. Don't you think so?"

Ted nodded his assent.

"Let's go over to the Days'. I want to see Mr. Day," Red Mack announced, as he finished combing his hair.

They found Mr. Day at home and glad to see them.

"Well, Mack, I suppose Ted has told you about his set-to with the kidnappers?"

Red looked his bewilderment.

"What kidnappers?" he ejaculated.

"Didn't he tell you?" the older man inquired. "Then I will."

When he had completed his account, his listener made no comment.

"Pretty brave and clever of him, wasn't it?" the speaker remarked, a little disappointed at Mack's lack of comment.

"Yes, it was," Red replied. "But you would expect Ted to do his best for his friends."

Somehow Ted liked his friend's comment even more than the fulsome praise of his other friends.

"Ted, suppose you go and see the captain about your affairs," Red Mack suggested. "In the meantime Mr. Day and I can talk over our plans."

"What plans have you in mind for Ted?" the older man inquired.

Whereupon his visitor went into details at once.

"If I can be of any service to you in any way, I shall be glad of it," Mr. Day announced when Red had completed the account of his plans.

"I suspect you may be of service. I think we may be able to tell in the next two months just how valuable our property will prove to be. If it is valuable and Arthur and I have to go to war, we shall ask you to have it developed. Will you?"

"Gladly," the older man replied.

The two talked further about the mine, Mr. Day, whose experience was in that line, asking many questions.

In the meantime, Ted had called on Captain Perkins. Upon the boy's entrance the captain had turned with a start.

"I was just thinking of you, Ted," he announced. "I've been assigned to Washington, in fact," he added blushing, "I am a major now."

"I'm glad," the boy answered simply.

"I was worried as to how I could take you with me. I don't know just how it can be done. The men at the camp have been assigned to their different regiments and—"

The captain paused, uncertain.

"Don't worry, captain. I just came to you about that very thing."

And then he told his friend of Red Mack's plans.

"I see," the officer replied slowly. "Perhaps it will not be a bad step for you. In all likelihood, it will not be for more than a month or so. Wish you luck. And tell Mack I should like to see him before he leaves."

"When do you go?" he added.

"Within the week," the boy replied.

THE RANGERS HAD RE-ESTABLISHED
RESPECT FOR AMERICA

"Then I'll be sure to see you again. You've been a big help to me, Ted. You'll make a good soldier if you do half as well as you did as a young soldier."

Ted returned to the hotel where he met Red Mack.

The end of the week found them on their way to Douglas.

Captain Payne was there. So was Arthur. The Rangers had continued their vigil of the border. Slowly the Mexicans under Villa and other outlaw jepes began to realize that these quiet, determined men who watched, patroled and guarded the interests of the border states were safest when undisturbed.

The Rangers had re-established respect for the things for which America stood.

The two, Mack and Ted, had taken the Mitchell for the trip, as Mr. Day had insisted that the car belonged to Ted. He did not add that he had deposited a bond with the sheriff to cover its value should a claim be made for it.

The party also rescued the old Ford which had served them so well when they opened the mine.

With the help of two Indians whom Mack had hired, the three, Red, Arthur and Ted set to work to prove the mine their road to prosperity.

What handicaps, adventures, misfortune and good fortune that followed in their footsteps, is told in the story of "Lucky the Young Navy Man."

Good Books for Boys and Girls

The Campfire Girls and Aunt Madge

The Campfire Girls' Week-End Party

Delightful stories that are sure to be well liked. The titles would indicate that they are purely girls' stories but boys will find them equally interesting. Be sure to read them.